ILLUMINATION
OF THE STONES

Other Titles by Art Ramsay
The Tibetan Wisdom Code
Seven Stones of Wisdom
Inner Peace Revealed

ILLUMINATION OF THE STONES

Art Ramsay, Ph.D.

MAGIC MOUNTAIN PRESS • ASHEVILLE, NC

Illumination Of The Stones
Book Three of the Wisdom Stones Trilogy
© 2014 by Art Ramsay, Ph.D.
All Rights Reserved

Magic Mountain Press
P.O. Box 1933
Asheville, NC 28802

Library of Congress Control Number: 2014936318
ISBN 978-0-9715946-3-0

Other Titles by Art Ramsay:

The Tibetan Wisdom Code © 2011, published by Magic Mountain Press.

Seven Stones of Wisdom, © 2007, published by Rampart Press Inc.

Inner Peace Revealed: Bringing Peace Into Your Everyday Life,© 2007 eBook

Cover and book design by Opus 1 Design, Los Angeles, CA

First Edition, May 2014

THIS BOOK IS DECICATED TO
MY EDITOR AND FRIEND
LaVonne Jordan

Who Has Been With Me Since The Beginning Of What Is Now
The Wisdom Stones Trilogy Thanks To Her Suggestion.

She Also Has Been My Fiction Writing Teacher
And Has Helped Me Get To The Level Of An Expert Writer.

ACKNOWLEDGEMENTS

After completing *The Tibetan Wisdom Code* and publishing it in 2011, the third book began its life through already started chapters on the last five Stones. During that time, I had many inquiries about when the third book would be published. My answer shifted a lot then due to illness and other changes in my life.

As with the first two books, my greatest teacher of what to leave in, take out, reword, character development, and so much more about fiction writing, was my editor and friend, LaVonne Jordan. The manuscript that I sent her in May, 2012 is very different from the book you have in your hands. What a journey those six months were.

After my last edit completion in December 2012, I sent the manuscript to my great friend of 40 years, Charlie Dutton. As always, he pointed out grammatical and other hard to spot errors. It is amazing what an author can miss repeatedly checking his own work.

Reverend Barbara Waterhouse, who also reviewed the first two books and wrote a blurb for the first one, gave me insight about the story's flow.

Pamela Terry of Opus 1 Design, who created a beautiful cover and great interior book layout. Given suggestions and photos of previous books, she developed a book design beyond what I had anticipated.

My publisher and friend, Karon Korp, president of Magic Mountain Press, found even more places to make changes and corrections in my manuscript during her edit. Through her guidance, the book is even better now than it was after all of the other updates.

Last but not least, my wife, Dee, for suggesting the title of this book. Without these people, I could not have produced a book of *Illumination Of The Stones'* quality, both inside and out.

INTRODUCTION

A synopsis of Book One and Book Two

n the first two books, we joined our adventurers, Emily, Greg, Karl, and later, Shannon as they first discovered a mission to find the Tibetan Wisdom Stones, and activate them so they could send spiritual energy into the world. In Book Two, they had to find a document that would keep the Stones energetically active. This book finishes their journey of finding and activating these special Wisdom Stones, begun in 2007, but planned centuries ago.

Seven Stones of Wisdom, the first book, begins the adventure in Sedona, Arizona. A mysterious blue stone shows up while the protagonist, Greg Frostburg, meditates. When he shows it to his girlfriend, Emily, she tells him it looks like a *Tibetan Wisdom Stone*. This mysterious revelation propels him into a venture called The Mission, to find six more Stones, hidden centuries before at sacred sites around the world.

Greg learns that *Tibetan Wisdom Stones* begin their life as normal stones, which are carefully selected by Tibetan monks. The stones are brought into a monastery where they are prayed and chanted over for months, or even years. They are then ready to accompany a monk, whenever he meditates and seeks connection with Spirit.

The Wisdom Stones found in the *Seven Stones of Wisdom* story had been prepared for a unique task – to give spiritual messages to the world and radiate sacred energy to heal a ravaged planet. Each Wisdom Stone is unique in shape, size, and color. Each stands for a particular aspect of the human psyche, and aids the listener in processing his or her own challenge with that aspect.

For example, the white Wisdom Stone stands for 'Acceptance', and gives the listener guidance to accept people and situations for what they are. As the adventurers travel to each site and find each Wisdom Stone, they are watched, and sometimes thwarted, in carrying out their mission. The powerful Catholic Church's Monsignor Terkenni gathers his band of henchmen, and sends them out to stop the group's dissemination of spiritual messages and energy. He cannot let go of the stranglehold the Church has had on its people for centuries.

The four comrades persevere, and The Mission is completed in Tibet, after many twists and turns, starts and stops and go's, along the way. We then find the team eighteen months later, enjoying the bliss of the buried Wisdom Stone's sacred energy. They have created a company that teaches spiritual principles more acceptable to the masses in a world that is slowly healing from the wounds of hatred, war, poverty, and racism.

The Tibetan Wisdom Code, the second book in the series, takes us on a new and mysterious journey when Emily becomes aware as Karl is informed that the Wisdom Stones are losing their energy. The only way to restore their energy is to locate a coded document, hidden in the early 1950's, in or near Tibet.

Their journey to find this mysterious document takes them to India, Tibet, Canada, Italy, and Bhutan. Their Ancient Wisdom Seminars business is interrupted by Monsignor Terkenni and his hired hit men known as The Cause, while these conspirators try to stop the group's spiritual teachings. Once Terkenni and his crew find out Greg and Emily are looking for a document that will make the Wisdom Stones more powerful, The Cause tries to stop their hunt for this important key.

Greg finally locates a document, only to find that it is just part of the full text. The story unfolds as Greg, Emily, and wise Tibetan Monks seek the complete document. Once found, they lose it again to The Cause, and Emily is kidnapped. They finally find and read the document, which tells them that there are five more Wisdom Stones to find and activate. This is where *Illumination Of The Stones* picks up their story in late summer of 2011.

PROLOGUE

Halmar Fitzburg stood at the front of a small, back room in a bar in Rome, Italy, speaking to a gathering of what was left of Monsignor Terkenni's renegades of The Cause. The room was lit by small lantern replicas hanging along the wooden walls, giving them a rich texture. With a tight grip of the podium, the tall German, formerly a general in the military, stared at the hand waving frantically. "You have a question?"

Kent Sourtaou stood; his huge body towered over his surroundings. "Yes ... sir. They have the wisdom book. What do we do now?" Saying 'sir' to someone did not feel right to Kent, but he was told by his new acquaintance, Friedrick, a member of Terkenni's group, The Cause, to be respectful to the German if he wanted to become a part of the group.

Fitzburg wrinkled his brow. "How do you know this?"

Kent stepped away from his chair. "My name is Kent Sourtaou, I worked for Terkenni and stole the book, but the American, Greg, got it back through trickery, when we met. He and his girlfriend, Emily, now have it and I believe it is in the United States."

"So you are the spy Monsignor Terkenni told me about?" The German gazed at Kent, who nodded. Fitzburg smiled. "You performed your task well, that is, until you allowed a person half your size to take it from you."

Kent caught Fitzburg's narrow gaze, his face flushed. "Yes sir." Kent sat down. *You pompous ass.*

Fitzburg put his hands on his hips. "Well that sort of thing will not happen again, will it Mr. Sourtaou?" Kent shook his head. "Good. Then we will work together to destroy that book and everything those misguided, godless heathens are doing. I know all of you, even though some of you may be new to me and The Cause. You would not be here if I had not already approved of your attendance. So do not think you can pull anything over on me. Is that clear?" Everyone nodded and said, "Yes sir."

"We have much to do." Fitzburg left the podium and paced in front of the room. "The Monsignor, as you know is in jail. I dare not visit him or I might wind up there also. So we must gather all the information we can to carry out our plan to stop whatever these people are trying to get away with. We will have to visit the United States and possibly Madrid again."

He returned to the podium and put his finger on a sheet of paper. "We have two main tasks – stop their barbarous teachings, and either find and destroy the book, or stop them when they travel to places to find more of these devil stones, as Monsignor Terkenni has called them. This venture will be tough and maybe dangerous, but we will prevail. How many are with me?"

All nine hands shot up. "Good. Let us now work out the details of who will do what."

1

SEDONA, AZ

The crystal blue Arizona sky stood out in contrast with the partially shaded sun, displaying its turquoise hues. The late summer weather had finished with its midsummer monsoons and settled into a pleasant mixture of beauty and warmth. Evening approached and a gentle cool breeze filled the air.

Emily Benson locked the door in the building where she held the Ancient Wisdom Seminars' classes, and strolled to her white, Toyota Camry car. She adjusted the student folders in her arm and stopped long enough to admire the sky. "Wow, Sedona unveils more mystical beauty every time I stop to discover it." Her gaze fell upon a group of red rocks just as the sun peeked through a cloud. "Amazing, the shades of red continue to astound me." She opened the car door and swished her long black hair to one side as she jumped into the seat for her short drive home.

Ten minutes later, Emily pulled into her garage and parked the car. She noticed an odd smell as she approached the garage's exit to the house. A chill crept down her spine and she stopped just short of the house's entry. "What is going on with me?" she mumbled to herself. When Emily finally opened the door, she entered the laundry room, and then froze in shock. "Oh, my god, what has happened?"

The laundry cabinets lay bare with their former contents strewn over the floor in front of her. She dropped the folders, and her black, velvet purse to wade through the mess and get to her kitchen. Emily found more disarray as she crept through food, liquids, and the cabinets' contents. Feeling fear grip her chest and stomach, she grabbed a large knife from the countertop and crept towards the small, square-shaped living room. While her Kung Fu black belt training could keep her out of trouble, she felt safer with the knife.

"Dudley, where are you boy?" She heard the movement of papers coming from the bedroom, and cautiously approached the doorway. She peeked around the corner, and saw her white and tan Himalayan cat push himself up from under a heap of scattered papers. She dropped the knife and pulled him into her arms. "You still know how to purr, attacked or not." Emily sat on the bare mattress with Dudley in her arms, surveyed piles of books and documents covering the floor of her bedroom. "I bet you were scared to death of whoever did this. Thank god you are safe."

Emily carried her fluffy cat back to the laundry room, got her cell phone from her purse, and called her business and romantic partner, Greg Frostburg. "My house is a mess. Someone has ransacked it." She burst into tears. "Please come over."

"Have you made sure there is no one there?" He asked with a worried voice.

Emily wrinkled her brow. "Yes, it is clear. But I need your support." He promised to be there soon and hung up.

She put the phone down, carried Dudley to the living room, and lay against the soft blue sofa. Emily glanced around the once stylish room at the torn curtains and slashed carpet. She closed her eyes feeling tightness in her chest, and tried to relax. *How could this happen?* She closed her eyes, took a few deep breaths, and tried to meditate, until Greg arrived. Her mind drifted back to a similar setting as a child. She had come home from school to find her family's living room in disarray and her mother lying on the floor. She shook her mother trying to wake her and then found blood. She screamed and ran to the phone and dialed 911, exactly as her mother had taught her. Emily turned and found a man standing over her. She screamed and ran outside. Suddenly, someone was shaking her. She opened her tear filled eyes.

"Emily, wake up, it's me, Greg."

She grabbed Greg and then held him tightly. Emily stopped trembling and crying after a few minutes in Greg's arms. "I remembered my mother's death sitting there before you arrived. Our house was in a similar mess back then. It brought back other memories too. I have a terrible feeling about this."

"Well, yeah I guess so. After all, your house has been ripped apart." Greg felt the tightness in her body, and even some in his own.

She pulled back and caught his gaze. His magical deep blue eyes held her gaze for a second. "My feeling is not about my house being wrecked. It is about who did it. My mom's house was razed because men were looking for something my dad had hidden."

"What has that got to do with…" Greg stopped and held her gaze, and then slowly shook his head with a grim smile. "Surely you don't mean?"

"Remember I told you the other day I have been having nightmares?" He nodded. "Well this morning I put the pieces together from what I had written in my journal. The dreams were about Terkenni and The Cause."

Greg shuffled around the room, his long, curly hair moving back and forth as he took in what she said. "That sounds like a big assumption. After all any thief, mind you a crazy one, could have been looking for something of value he or she thought was here." He put his hands on his hips. "But reliving that moment of terror back then surely brought it to the fore. So you think it was The Cause searching for something – like the Wisdom Stone Book?"

"Bingo. You've got it." Emily wrinkled her brow. "This is what is so disturbing. Not that my house has been wrecked, but that

The Cause is at it again; ready to try to stop us no matter what. It has been only a little over a month since we left Italy, after I was rescued from Terkenni's clutches; and now we have five Wisdom Stones to find."

Silence crept into the room. Only Dudley's gentle purr filled the air. Greg sat next to the cat and ran his hand over the soft fur. "So putting Terkenni and his men in jail has stopped nothing. Evidently The Cause has been reformed by Halmar Fitzburg."

Emily stared at him. "Where is the book?"

"Ah, hidden in my house. Why?" Greg got up.

Emily's eyes grew wide. "Because they may be searching your house now."

Greg's mouth dropped open, and they both ran to his car.

2

SEDONA, AZ

The sun set low on Sedona's horizon sprinkling a rainbow of colors through the sky. Karl Josephon, the third partner of Ancient Wisdom Seminars, stood on the patio of his gray and white condominium enjoying the overhead display of colors. He turned and hurried inside to the ringing phone, and pulled it to his ear.

"Hi Karl, we have discovered a serious problem. Emily and I are at my house now and called to be sure you were okay." Greg said.

Karl felt concerned. "Ah, what kind of serious problem?"

Greg told him of Emily's house and that they were at his place now. "We have found nothing amiss here, but it may only be a matter of time, before yours or my place is tossed. We need to get together and sort out our next steps."

"Come on over here, and we can discuss what our next move might be. " Karl said.

Greg paused, "I have to finish packing for my trip to Calcutta tomorrow, but after that we will be over." Ending the call, he refocused on his luggage.

Karl moved to the kitchen, and prepared his evening meal.

Back at Greg's house, Emily said, "That was fast."

Greg took a deep breath. "I know, but someone could be listening. I don't want to give away our plans and time schedule. We'll fix things here and then visit Karl. I have a special place to hide this." He removed the Wisdom Stone Book from a shelf in his living room bookcase and moved to the bedroom.

"Can I look?" Emily smiled and followed Greg.

When he got to the bedroom, Greg removed a piece of wood from just under the bed, placed the book carefully within the hole, and then recovered it. "There, that should be hidden enough."

Emily inspected the floor and ran her hands over it. "Pretty nifty. I can't tell there is a hole there, and I just watched you move its covering. That should keep their snooping at bay."

"Best I can do. But really, do we even need the book anymore." Greg gave her a quizzical look. "I mean we know there are five new Stones to find, that the first place to search is Stonehenge, and that at each site after that we will be given directions for the next location."

Emily wrinkled her brow. "Hmm, maybe you are right. Still…" She wrapped her arms around him. "Okay, I agree."

Greg finished packing for his trip in the morning to Calcutta, and then the two of them drove to Karl's.

As Greg ascended the steps at Karl's condo, he paused and then glanced around the street below. "Can't be too careful." He weakly smiled.

"Hi, Karl," Emily said as he opened the door. She hugged him, barely getting her arms around his wide frame. "I know we had planned to get together tonight to discuss our financial situation, but my wrecked house sort of got in the way."

Karl smiled. "Yeah, a 'wrecked house thing' can really be annoying." They laughed.

After discussing this recent incident in their relationship with The Cause, they focused on their present Mission, and traveling to five new sacred sites, finding a Wisdom Stone at each one, and their activation.

"They must know we have more Stones to find, so they will be hot on our heels to stop us from helping the Recipient find and activate each new Stone. It's kind of funny how they want to stop us, specifically, but it is the Recipient who will ultimately find and activate the Stones; all we are doing is helping him or her do the work and be guards."

Karl smiled and caught Greg's gaze ... "Well we will know more on your return, won't we?"

The next morning, Greg put his bag in the trunk, and climbed in the front seat of Emily's Camry. The ride was quiet until Emily asked, "The house is safe. Right?"

"By safe you mean no hoodlums can easily break in and steal the Wisdom Stone Book?"

She glared at Greg for a moment. "You know what I mean. Should I be riding over there everyday to make sure no one is considering an act of 'search and destroy'?"

"Whatever you choose. But I would suggest trusting the Universe and go about your business."

She pulled into the airport parking garage. "I see your point."

After leaving Greg at his gate, Emily returned to her car and drove home to West Sedona. *Well, Emily what do you do about that book? It is hidden under a floorboard. Seems safe enough to me. Get over it.* After she arrived home, she settled into cleaning up her house. Later, that evening she sat in her swivel chair in her small office and went over her preparations for the class she would teach in the morning just as the phone rang. She noted the caller id.

"Hi, Karl, what's up?"

Karl's voice sounded strange. "Did you forget about our meeting?"

"Oh, damn, I'm sorry Karl. I guess cleaning up the mess here tore it from my memory. I'll be right over." She grabbed her briefcase and put the lesson plans on top of the financial ledger prepared two days ago, and made her way to the garage. On her way to Karl's condo, she thought about how things had changed in the past three months.

She stopped in front of the condo and then made her way to the ornamental front door. Once inside, Karl served some green tea, and then sat at the kitchen table. "You okay after yesterday's ordeal? You look a bit troubled."

"I was just thinking about our arduous encounters the past couple of months, and how I am not ready to repeat them so soon." Emily held the cup near her lips. "I think the thing yesterday triggered something. On the way here I was thinking that we went from a team of business people and teachers, to hunting for that mysterious Wisdom Stone book."

She sighed. "How blissful we were hanging out together, teaching spiritual principles, and watching our seminar business grow. Then, boom, the Stones lost power and the hunt began. But," she smiled, "Terkenni was caught stealing from his church and leading renegades to stop us. Now, here we are ready for another venture to sacred sites searching for even more Wisdom Stones. I guess we create what we come here to do. I'll be okay. I am just wondering, am I ready for yet another encounter with The Cause?"

"I guess I haven't thought much about it lately; been busy with business." Karl leaned back in the large-chair. "The situation you encountered yesterday certainly was powerful enough to trigger plenty of old stuff, especially with the possibility of another visit from our nemesis. You okay to discuss business matters?" She nodded.

Since Karl handled the finances of Ancient Wisdom Seminars, Emily showed him her projected expenditures for the next six months. "Of course, this might have to be modified depending on what we spend getting to sacred sites, and hunting for Wisdom Stones. The Wisdom Stone book told us there are five more Stones to find and activate. That means travel to five places somewhere in the world. The only one we know about now is England."

"That aspect troubles me, because we may not be able to do both." Karl rubbed his brow. "We have already spent money we hadn't planned for, finding the Wisdom Stones Book. And then there was the down time after the explosion in Madrid, with no money coming in. We are still paying Isabel as a guard in Madrid." He looked up. "Didn't you say something about the possibility of her joining you and Greg during the Wisdom Stone search?"

Emily pushed her chair back. "It was a thought. I am not sure it will happen. If The Cause turns up, and I am sure they will, she might be valuable in fending off attacks, while we hunt for the Stones. They may not know what we are up to this moment, but Fitzburg was close to Terkenni, so he most likely knows a lot about what our plans are."

"As long as we are paying her, we might as well use her where she is most needed." Karl poured more tea in their cups. "If The Cause is focused on stopping you and Greg from activating more Wisdom Stones, they probably will not be trying to blast holes through our classrooms."

Emily shrugged. "We'll see. Right now, Greg is on his way to Calcutta to set our search in motion. We should know in a few days how all of the facets fit together. Right now we have classes to teach."

They finished their discussion, and Emily left. When she arrived home, she found a note taped to her door. It read, "We are watching you."

3

CALCUTTA, INDIA

alcutta had not changed since Greg visited The Council three months ago. Of course, a centuries old city wouldn't be expected to change in only a few months. On his way from the hotel, he passed the enchanting Kalighat Temple, with its white domed spire and colorful walls. It gave him the feeling of a tourist, while his taxi drove along the nearby Hooghly River.

Greg left the vehicle and climbed the long flight of wooden stairs, on the side of a red brick building, where members of The Council met. The building seemed different somehow. The walls looked cleaner, and had on a fresh odor. Had it gotten a facelift? Greg knocked on the heavy wood door. A man dressed in a white, silken blouse and black billowy pants met him. As he entered the room lit only by seven oil lamps along the white, concrete walls, a round table occupied by eight men awaited him.

"Welcome, young Greg," said Nocunda, the Council's leader. "We have anxiously awaited your arrival." He motioned for Greg to sit next to him. "Tell us about your adventures in Tibet and the marvelous book you found."

Greg smiled. "Well, you know most of the tale, don't you? For we have kept you informed.'

"Yes, you are right." Nocunda smiled. "Perhaps one of our members can give us a quick summation, so that we all know the story. And you can answer questions about your personal experiences."

A man dressed in a tan and black business suit stood. "I have some questions, but first, a brief story of what I know." Natcur said. "You look for a book to help seven Wisdom Stones from losing energy, and so find the first part of this Wisdom Stone Book in Lhasa. Then you get a secret letter, decode it, and that led you to Bhutan at Gaza monastery. There you discover part two of a book that tells you of five more Stones, and how they must be found and activated by 11-11-2011. My question is this – how did you feel about Emily's kidnapping and your own amnesia?"

Greg leaned forward. "I was afraid for her life to be honest. I had no idea what Terkenni was capable of. It was a relief to hear her voice once more. As to my encounter with the blow by Kent, it was like being in two different worlds; like being in two dreams, not knowing which one was real. It was scary."

The group thanked Natcur and Greg for the recap. Then Greg continued. "I am here today to receive the name of the first Recipient. Since we only know the location of the first site, which I am sure you are aware, is Stonehenge, in England, I need to confirm who we will meet there, help find the Stone, and perform the Activation ceremony."

"Yes, of course you do." Nocunda bowed slightly. The Indian had always been polite and honored his culture's customs. "The Source spoke to me last evening and gave me this name and how to contact him." He slid a piece of paper toward Greg. "The man has no knowledge of what is about to unfold in his life, as were the others you contacted for the first Mission. I know he will be in knowledgeable and loving hands when he meets with you and Emily. One more thing about the site; even though the Activation Ceremony will take place at Stonehenge, the Stone's location is not so clear. It is in the area, but not necessarily at Stonehenge."

Greg stared at Nocunda. "Not at Stonehenge, but nearby. Did I hear you correctly?" The man nodded. "Okay, thanks for the warning. We will have to allow for that." He picked up the paper and examined it. "Master Wu. Sounds Asian."

"Yes, but as you can see, he currently lives in England with his son." Nocunda leaned into the tall-backed chair.

"Is there anything I need to know about Master Wu, before we meet with him?" Greg faced The Council members.

A man with white hair and beard bowed. "We know only that he teaches Kung Fu with his son at their school near London. He is not yet aware of the mission he is about to begin."

"Thank you." Greg bowed. "I have one other request. We are running low on funds and will need some help very soon. Can The Council assist us or guide us to an organization that can?"

Nocunda smiled. "We anticipated your request and have already contacted your financial officer, Karl. We will support your endeavor as long as we can."

Greg took a deep breath and sat back in his chair. "Thank you all. We will not let you down. We will not let the world down."

The group discussed the details of travel and accommodations. They also got into a debate about The Cause, and what it might take to thwart their moves to stop Emily, Greg and the Recipient at each site. "But remember," said Nocunda. "No one will know the location, nor the Recipient of the next site until after the prior Activation ceremony."

Greg nodded. "Yes, we need to keep this secret."

Nocunda smiled. "We join you in keeping the secret intact." The rest of the group nodded. They finished the meeting with a long meditation to honor the new Mission and its players, but mostly to assure their safety and success. Afterwards, the group adjourned to a different part of the building where they enjoyed Indian snacks and drink. It provided Greg time to get reacquainted.

Later, as Greg left the building and made his way down the short alley-like street to the main boulevard, he felt like someone was watching him. An eerie feeling came over him and he glimpsed a dark figure in the shadows. He broke into a run and hailed a cab.

4

ROME, ITALY

our men sat around a corner table in the dimly lit bar on the outskirts of Rome, Italy. Halmar Fitzburg read a note from one of his comrades in the United States. "This is my first communication from Jesse and the other two positioned near Sedona, Arizona."

"We have watched the movements of the woman, called Emily Benson, the last three days. Her partner, Greg Frostburg, lives separately, and is currently traveling in India. She began teaching a class today and will most likely continue for the remainder of the week. We encountered some difficulty on our first visit to her place of residence. Even though we searched every inch of her home, we could not find any trace of the book you seek. We have not approached the other two residences as yet. Awaiting your orders about our next move."

"We are ready to take our next step." Fitzburg bent forward. "I have sent three men to Madrid, Spain to determine whether we can gather any information there that would be useful in stopping these hellions."

Kent Sourtaou raised his hand. "I would like to go to Sedona to spy on that guy Greg Frostburg. I have a score to settle with him."

"Settling scores is not important right now," Fitzburg said. "We have to stop them from doing whatever they are planning. That is your first and most important activity. If you manage to settle your score while stopping him, then so be it. You will have your chance in time. When they visit the first place to find stones, we will be there to stop them. Our priority is to uncover the location of that site. You will be more valuable to this project at the site than in Arizona. In the meantime, we have training to do. "

Kent leaned forward. "Okay, I understand and look forward to my encounter with them. Just how are we going to find out where this first site will be?"

"We have ways." Fitzburg moved to a chart. "We must monitor their conversations, first, by telephone, but also through distant listening devices so that we can hear conversations in their houses. These will give us what we want without having to visit them in person. If these devices fail to give us what we need, there are other ways."

Friedrick raised his hand. "How are we going to listen to their telephone conversations?"

"I am a retired military general, remember?" Fitzburg smiled. "I have access to satellite and other monitoring equipment. We just tune in to their frequencies and locations with those devices. I do not personally do this, but my comrades in Munich are there for me when I call. We get the information they send to us, or we listen in to one of their interceptions, and we have our information."

Kent banged his hand on the table. "Wow, that sounds complicated."

"What we must do now is plan first how we will interact with Munich, what we will do with the data we collect, and our next moves after getting this information. I have given my comrades the three addresses of these people in Sedona. They will use the physical addresses, names, and other information to pinpoint the phone numbers. Each of you will have specific jobs within the overall plan of stopping their activities. That will be our main focus. We also must begin shutting down those classes. But that is secondary and can wait until we have stopped them from finding more of those stones."

Kent held up a glass of beer. "To our success in stopping them freaks."

The other men held up their glasses as well. The general nodded, and they all drank their beer together as a sign of commitment.

5

SEDONA, AZ

Emily and Karl sat on a blue knitted sofa across from Greg in his adobe house in West Sedona, Arizona. He had collected the necessary information from The Council about the first site, and the person who would be the Recipient there. The three were now ready to plan their journey to England.

"Stonehenge has always been a mystery to me," said Greg. "There are so many theories. I visited the site years ago, before they put barriers around the stones to keep people from touching them. Of course, the barriers are only ropes, but are sufficient to keep people away. I actually did touch the stones and felt their energy. We will have to resort to our previous stories of archeological exploration as to why we need to explore 'non-public' areas of the site."

Emily brought a tray of chai tea to the teak coffee table, and then filled three earthen cups. "Yes, but we will have to contact each site at the time we are given the name and location, rather than weeks before the trip as we did for the first Mission. But I am sure Karl can take care of that with ease." She smiled.

"An easy task." Karl stirred his tea. "Site managers are eager to attract groups and scientific study to these places. We need only convince them that our work is valid and will enhance public knowledge of them."

Greg slid a paper across the table to Karl. "Here is the information about Master Wu that you will need to contact him and set a date for our exploration at Stonehenge. Once that is done, we are good to go."

"Yes, most of the Recipients eagerly accepted their tasks on the first Mission." Karl took the paper. "Since we will not have the lead-time we had before, the date chosen will not give them as much time to prepare for the trip to the site both physically and emotionally. But it will work out just fine, I am sure."

Emily sat back holding her cup. "By the time I finish this week's class, you should have everything in place, Karl. Greg can work on what we need to take, getting there and back, and prepare for running into The Cause."

"Yeah, that last item might be our most difficult task." Greg clasped his hands together. "They have a new leader, who seems to be more impulsive than Terkenni, based on his blowing up classrooms and such just months ago. This could work for, or against us. We will have to be alert and ready for anything." Greg stood with his cup held out in front of him. "Let's do this thing." The other two stood and touched their cup to his.

"While we are face to face, I want to reveal to you a very important message The Source told me as I was leaving the building there." Greg turned his head and checked the only window in the room, and then lowered his voice to a whisper. "I do not even want to say this in a whisper, so just read this." He unrolled a piece of paper and held it up for the other two to read.

"I will explain this more when we get to England."

6

LONDON, UK

ain pelted the covered porch of the Chinese-styled house in northwest London. Colorful screens kept the rain out, allowing Master Wu to perform his morning practice. While practicing Kung Fu in the rain had its merits, he opted to keep his white warrior robe dry. He completed five sessions, and then chose his Shaolin Longevity sword. It had been in his family for centuries and its character gave him a feeling of power.

After completing his Kung Fu session, Master Wu sat in meditation for an hour, as was his practice each morning. His meditation seemed different today; he had a vision of Stonehenge and participating in some kind of event that would affect the whole world. As he arose, he bowed. "I am willing to take part in whatever you have prepared for me, Master."

Wu then joined his son, Jon, for breakfast. He had come to live with Jon a decade ago, from Dengfeng in the Shaolin Province. His son had created a school of Kung Fu five years earlier, and had asked his dad to join him as the Master Instructor. Master Wu had agreed, but it took four years to break away from his own business and family ties. By the time he arrived in London, he had learned English well and had no problem communicating with the students.

"What have you planned for today, father?" Jon passed the rice.

The Master bowed and took the bowl. "It is a day of venture, I think. I go for a walk in the forest."

Jon laughed. "Forest? There is no forest in London. You are meaning the park, yes?"

"It is what you make it, my son." He first caught Jon's gaze, and then stared out of the window overlooking his garden. "What is a forest, but a dense wood? Cannot my thicket of berry bushes be a forest to Chen Chin?" He nodded toward their Siamese cat lying in his cozy bed.

Jon smiled. "Of course, father. I am too Westernized, I suppose, and view words literally."

"Ah, yes, Westernized." Master Wu sat back in the wood and metal chair. "That is why we sit up here on these stoles, and rest our weary bones at this table. But here we are in London and we must live as the 'Romans', yes?" He got up, bowed, and then shuffled to the front door. "See you later, gator." He laughed and left the house.

Master Wu paused, stretched, noted that the rain had stopped, and then strutted across the street. He reached the park ten minutes later and slowed his pace. *And now we enter the forest.* He bowed to a group of trees off to one side, and proceeded down the sidewalk into the park. Master Wu gravitated toward his favorite trail and whistled a little. Patches of noon sun came through the clouds and splattered shades of yellow and white across his face and arms.

After a one hour jaunt through the park, where he once again marveled at the colorful birds, scampering squirrels, rabbits, and all sorts of plants and trees, Master Wu sat beside a small lake. Ripples, caused by swans and other birds, interrupted the smooth water and reflections of clouds and bits of blue sky. His mind quieted, and he settled into a trance. *Ignore not, your power.* A voice came through his mind. *You are ready to step into a new role. You are called. The human race is ready for a new world. Begin now.*

The Kung Fu Master had been called many times during his life to step into a new task that challenged him and took him to the edge. *I am ready.* He bowed, came back into awareness of the birds around him, and opened his eyes. He arose, shook out his limps, and continued his hike through the park. Thirty minutes later, he arrived back at his son's house.

Jon met him just as he entered the small entryway. "Father, a man named Karl Josephon called from the United States. He said it was very important that you contact him as soon as possible." He handed his father the notepad where he had jotted Karl's number.

Wu took the paper and gave it a curious look. "Did he say what this important matter is about?" Jon shook his head. "I must make contact with this man then with much haste; after I have my repast, that is." He drank some iced water, and then fixed a rice bowl with vegetables. After enjoying his meal, Master Wu made the phone call, curiosity filling his mind.

"Hello, this is Master Wu calling from London to speak with Mr. Karl Josephon, please."

The voice coming through the phone informed him that he had reached Karl and that they had important business to discuss. Karl told him about the Wisdom Stones and filled him in on how the first seven were found and put in place. "We now have five more to find and activate, and you are one of the five chosen to do that. My business partners, Emily and Greg, will meet with you and explain the situation in detail. Meanwhile, you will need to take leave of what you are now doing for approximately two weeks or so, and devote yourself full time to finding this first Wisdom Stone of what we call Mission 2. Do you understand?"

Master Wu's heart raced with excitement and anticipation. "Yes, I have awaited your call." The phone went silent for a moment.

"Ah, you have awaited my call?" said Karl. "How did you know I would call?"

Master Wu relaxed into the cushioned chair. "I have vision."

"Well, we are most happy for you to agree to carry out this task." Karl realized that the man was short on words and did not want to prolong the conversation. He finished explaining when and how Emily and Greg would meet with him, and ended the call.

Master Wu set down the phone, strolled to the kitchen, and fixed some green tea. "Father, what did the man say?"

"I am to go on a secret mission at Stonehenge. It may be fun." Master Wu smiled.

"But, you do not know these people. There might be danger." Jon said.

The Master put his cup on the table. "If I face danger, it is not from the people that will join me. Have you not faced danger when challenging an opponent in the finals? The 'Kill of Death' tournament is filled with danger, yes?"

Jon nodded. "Okay, you win father. I trust your judgment. If I can be of any help, let me know."

"Yes, when the people who want to stop this Mission show up, it may get challenging. We will stay in touch."

7

MADRID, SPAIN

The morning sun lit the patio of Shannon McKinksley's stucco house near Madrid, Spain. Her red hair gave off an auburn tint from the sun's light. Across the table from her sat Isabel Frekni, the Italian Kung Fu martial arts master that Ancient Wisdom Seminars had hired to keep The Cause at bay. Colorful plants surrounded the patio and the fragrance blossoms lifted their spirits. "Where did you find this necklace?" Shannon asked while she examined the piece.

"At the edge of the wooded area behind the classroom. It must have been dropped during my scuffle with the 'bomb squad' of The Cause." Isabel stirred her coffee. "Since it has the initials H.F. on the back of the locket, I figured it might belong to that German guy."

"You do have a way with words." Shannon smiled, and turned the gold locket over revealing the initials. She opened it. "My, what a pretty little girl. It might be Fitzburg's daughter or granddaughter. What do you think?"

"That is the conclusion I came to also, but I had a more sinister thought about how we might use it." Isabel smiled.

"Oh, and what might that be?" asked Shannon.

Isabel put her cup back in the saucer. "We kidnap her and hold her, to threaten Fitzburg like Terkenni did with Emily. Make him give up trying to stop the Mission Greg and Emily are about to begin, or never see her again."

"Wow, that is intense." Shannon placed the necklace on the table. "I don't know whether Emily, Karl, and Greg would go for that. Kidnapping is illegal. Besides, from both a business standpoint of teaching spiritual principles, and as spiritual teachers and healers, it goes against everything we stand for."

Isabel picked up the necklace. "I agree it is a rash move, and I do not suggest it is tried right away, nor for us to tangle with the law. But if things get out of hand with The Cause, it might be a bargaining chip."

"I see your point," said Shannon. "I will pass on your suggestion to Karl. In the meantime, I have a class to start tomorrow. Thanks to you, I am really getting proficient at Kung Fu. Can we have another session this afternoon?"

Isabel smiled. "I am always ready to help you better your defensive maneuvers. You never know when The Cause might try to blow up something again. By the way, what is this class about that begins tomorrow?"

"Thank you, Isabel, you have been a great help in the last few weeks." Shannon finished her coffee and reached for the carafe. "More coffee?" Isabel nodded. "This class begins the student's journey of Personal Responsibility. It follows the first classes introducing them to spiritual principles and how they work in their lives. It is a great subject to begin this next series."

"I was thinking the other night that it might be helpful to the students if you were to teach some Kung Fu moves to those interested, after each class. That way, you would get a chance to teach again, and they would benefit from it."

Isabel sat back, pushing the metal chair away from the table. "That does sound interesting. Let me consider how that would work. I will let you know tomorrow." She noted the time. "I need to get downtown and pick up a few things."

"Good. I also have to get going with class preparation for tomorrow morning. We can meet then. Oh, one more thing. Emily mentioned that they might need your assistance when they visit the first site. I told them as long as your duties guarding the classroom are not needed, it would be okay with me. She would like you to consider it." Shannon and Isabel stood simultaneously.

"Okay, I will let you know. It sounds exciting to visit a sacred site." Isabel hugged Shannon and left.

Shannon cleared the table, carried the cups to the kitchen sink, and visited the office area she had set up in her spare bedroom. She placed the class manual on the walnut desk, and settled into the wood and cloth chair. This class, Shannon realized, was fueled by questions and answers, so it may prove more challenging to carry out. There are no pat answers, since everyone has a different perspective about life. She could only give her Ancient Wisdom Seminar's view of where we are going, and what to look for. Shannon leaned forward and wrote notes along the borders of the pages.

Would this class be effective based on what she had written from the outline Emily had given her, and the additional content of questions and answers? Tired, Shannon leaned back in the chair and closed her eyes. A vision flashed through her mind of one of the most terrifying experiences she ever had. *She was curled up in the fetal position on the floor of a jeep, hanging on to Karl's jacket. Bullets hit the back and side of the vehicle as the tough Aussie sped around hairpin curves on the steep side of the Australian mountain. She could feel the two right wheels leave the pavement, while making the last curve. Her breaths came faster as she thought each one would be her last. A crash behind them sounded as if the other vehicle had left the road.* Then Shannon almost fell from the chair and her eyes popped open.

She caught herself and then looked up at the tiled ceiling and trembled. "Oh my God, I was back in Australia with Karl and

Chris; he had the turquoise Stone of Harmony. What caused that? Is harmony the attribute coming up for me? Or is it something I must teach tomorrow in addition to my outline? Wow, what an insight."

Shannon got up and strolled to the kitchen and poured a glass of water. "Wait a minute. If that insight was about harmony, why was it about the chase? Why not the Activation? Maybe this needs more scrutiny Shannon." She moved out onto the patio and settled into a lounge chair. "Let's see. What is the opposite of harmony?" She placed a pad of paper on her lap and wrote: chaos, discord, separation. She discounted chaos and discord, figuring they presented no real-life lessons, but separation from one another causes discord, so chose separation as the opposite of harmony, and 'harmony versus separation' as that session's title. *This, I think is what that vision is telling me; we cannot experience both simultaneously. We can't feel separate from each other and live in harmony.* She integrated the harmony/discord piece into the first class's outline.

In the evening, Shannon and Isabel got together for some Kung Fu lessons and practice.

The students assembled in the small classroom, in a quaint little town just outside of Madrid. The room had no windows, and only wood paneled walls. Even though it was small, its high ceiling and openness kept the twenty desks from seeming cramped. They all seemed happy to continue their study of how life really works. Shannon introduced herself and noted that most of the students had been in the last class. There were two she did not recognize, and had everyone introduce themselves so that the newer attendees would feel comfortable.

Outside, Isabel roamed the perimeters of the property surrounding the classroom building. Nothing seemed out of the ordinary in the grassy area that had been cleared to construct the sturdy white brick building. The tall, muscular woman, wearing loose dark pants and shirt meandered into the wooded area, where she had found the necklace a month ago. Tire tracks were still present. It made her wonder about how Fitzburg knew the location of the building. *I guess with so much information available on the internet, anyone can find anything easily; scary.* She explored the area thoroughly seeking any clues to help her know more about the culprits that might show up again at any moment. Finding nothing, Isabel brushed back her black hair tied in a ponytail, and wandered back to the classroom area and sat in the shade.

"Since this is the second class of Ancient Wisdom Seminar's first course, I will spend some time this morning reviewing the last class's content. Then, we will move into new a new lesson." Shannon picked up a manual from her desk. "Some of the content in each class is fueled by your questions from previous classes, and so it will be this afternoon. Let's get started."

"There are two ideas or states of mind that were mentioned during the first session: separation and harmony." Shannon wrote them on the white board. "Now there are others, but for today, I want to focus on these two, because they are opposites. Harmony in music gives us melodic sounds that lift us while listening to them. Harmony in life is similar to how nature works. When we walk through a forest, we notice how the creatures that live there and the plants that surround them live so well together. Each has its function, both for itself and for the good of the whole." Shannon then circled 'separation'.

"Separation, on the other hand, plays a very different role in our lives. When each of us feels like we are separate from everyone else, we lose the possibility of coming together in a harmonious way. Now the question that came up, and what you are probably thinking right now is 'aren't we really separate?' Look, you have a body, I have a body; they are not joined. Yes, that is how it looks, and from a purely physical standpoint, you are right. But, we are not just bodies. Our bodies are vehicles for us to explore this physical world; we truly are spiritual beings inhabiting this planet through our bodies."

A hand shot up near the front. "So you are saying that my body is like my automobile, I understand that. But could I not move around here without a body, like a ghost?" Some of the others laughed.

Shannon smiled. "Well, yes I guess you could. But what could you accomplish? You see, we are here in bodies for a reason. They give us a way to do things, the actions we came here to do, to accomplish a purpose we could not have done without bodies. This is completely off the subject and I do not want to spend time on this now. This is how we get material for future class sessions. I will make note of it and see if I can fit it in before the end of the week." She jotted some notes on her pad.

"Getting back to the discussion, we have a choice to act out our belief in separation, or we can recognize that we are billions of bodies that affect one another in everything we do, say, and even think. Of course, it is not only our bodies that are doing these actions, it is the consciousness that lives through our bodies; and this is where our connections join and bring us harmony. Let's take a break."

During the break, Shannon called Karl to inquire how plans were progressing for Emily and Greg's visit to the first site. There was no answer, so she left a message. When the students returned, she continued the lesson about choosing harmony or separation.

"Now that we have seen the huge difference between harmony and separation, let us look at how that plays out in our lives." Shannon moved through the classroom while she talked, using her arms to emphasize ideas. "When we bring harmony into our lifestyle, a world opens that we may have not seen before. People are friendlier, processes go smoother, our bodies feel more energetic, and a whole host of other benefits appear. How unlike a mindset of separation this is. You already know and have experienced that separation brings fear, hate, judgment, racism, and profound disconnection with each other." She stopped in front of the class.

"Do you see now how choosing to live harmoniously can change your life?" Most of the students nodded, others just seemed to contemplate the idea. Shannon held a question and answer session, providing more examples of harmony and separation. The students left for the day, satisfied they had learned a valuable and applicable lesson.

Later that evening, after her meal and a Kung Fu session with Isabel, she sat with a cup of herbal tea and relaxed. As she brought the cup to her mouth, her cell phone played its cheery tune.

"Hi, Shannon," Emily said. "It looks like you are the main teacher, so to speak, for awhile. We will check in with you when we get to Stonehenge. If it appears we need Isabel, we will let you know. It looks like Mission 2 is ready to role."

8

ROME, ITALY

Halmar Fitzburg *tapped his fingers on the large, rectangular* table in the 'party room' of a bistro in downtown Rome. Four of the nine men he had hired to stop Mission 2 sat with him drinking beer. "Tonight we celebrate the beginning of the end," he gave them an evil smile. "The beginning of our Cause to end those misguided heroes' mission, and their stones of hell." He held up his beer mug. The others did the same as they clinked together.

"I have a report from our fellow members in Madrid." Fitzburg read from the sheet of paper. "The teacher is in the classroom with twenty students. The guard roams the perimeter and stopped to investigate the area where you parked your truck when we tried to plant the second bomb two months ago. She seemed to be looking for something. Nothing else to report."

"I also have gotten word from our men in Sedona. They used the amplified listening devices to spy on one of the houses. The three fiends met there, and discussed their venture. They are going to Stonehenge in England." Halmar shifted in his chair. "We will meet them there." He caught Kent's gaze. "You now will have the opportunity to encounter your adversary and get your revenge."

Kent smiled. *Oh, how good that will feel.*

"Tell us, Kent, what your quarrel is with Mr. Frostburg." The general leaned back.

The other men turned toward Kent, seated at the end of the table. They seemed interested in hearing from one of their comrades, perhaps to compare their own stories with his.

"Like I said before, he got the drop on me and with the help of his monk friends, and took the book." Kent said. "But worse, they tied my body so I could hardly walk, and ended up taking me to jail, where I spent 30 days in a dark cell. They fed me awful Chinese food, and not enough to feed a girl. That is why I want to tear his head off when I catch up with him."

Fitzburg leaned forward. "All good reasons. But in case you have not recognized some lessons to learn here, let me tell you what you need to do next time you meet him or anyone you think you can beat easily. First, a smaller man can move fast and get to areas around you that you might not be aware of in your haste to conquer. Second, you seemed to have given up once you were tied, which you could have avoided with some focused, extra effort. All in all, do not be so confident, because you are big, that you cannot lose."

Kent lowered his head. "Yes sir, I see that now. Thanks."

"I remember a few years ago having a similar experience." Gedof put his glass on the table. The stocky German wore an angry face and squeezed his muscular hands together. "I was in this tavern down in Wiesbaden, and these two American soldiers got really out of control. They started getting loaded and wrecking things. I was working as an assistant manager of the place that night, and tried to stop them. But they got worse and called me a kraut, and then took some swings at me and another guy helping out. One of them was big, like you Kent, and the other was much smaller, about my size. I was able to duck under the big guy's swings and tackle him from below, but the smaller guy was harder to deal with. The two of us, with some other help, finally threw them out, but not easily. So size can fool you sometimes."

The general nodded.

"I tell you, if I had to go up against a guy like you, Kent, I would run the other way." Said Pilgroy. They all laughed.

"Just remember," said Fitzburg. "You all will face opponents that seem easy to beat, and others that seem unbeatable. But in the end, it is not how big or small they are, it is how careful you are in carrying out the attack or defense against them. Brains win more than brawn most of the time, and that is how we will outwit our enemies when we meet them in England." He held up his glass. "To victory no matter what."

The rest stood, held up their glasses and shouted, "Victory!"

9

ENGLAND

As Emily and Greg left London Heathrow airport in their rental car, Greg fumed about driving on the "wrong side of the road." "I always have difficulty getting used to the traffic patterns in other countries," he said, gripping the wheel tighter. "But switching lanes is the most irritating. I always have wondered why some countries chose the right side of the road to drive on and others chose the left. Well, at least it is only a short drive to Salisbury."

"I always wanted to visit Salisbury anyway," Emily said, glancing out the windows. "I am glad it is our rendezvous point with Master Wu. It will be exciting."

Greg drove onto the M3 Motorway and left the burgeoning city behind. "Well it won't be so exciting when The Cause shows up, especially if what The Source said is true about Kent joining them. I really don't want to tangle with this guy, Kent, again. I have to laugh. Even though a couple of months ago, he caused me to have two weeks of memory loss, not to mention pain, and set up your kidnapping, *he* wants to get back at me for sending him to jail; go figure."

"Well, that is the way the criminal mind works, dear." Emily gazed out of the window at the farmland and stone fences.

Greg shook his head. "Well, at least I know he might show up. So I can prepare. That guy is big. How I managed to outmaneuver him before may prove that size is not so important when it comes to martial arts, but one misstep on my part, and I'm toast."

"We are both black belt Kung Fu warriors." Emily smiled. "We will do fine. Besides, isn't Master Wu a Kung Fu master?"

Greg shrugged. "I guess; thus the name, 'Master' Wu. But, whatever, Kent is after me; I am his target." He pulled off the Motorway, onto the A303. "Almost there. I could sure use a meal."

Thirty minutes later, they pulled into the hotel parking lot, and then checked in. The hotel looked rustic with modern-day upgrades. The ground floor had wooden walls, ceilings and floors with embedded carvings that appeared to be a century or more old.

Over a light snack, they discussed plans for meeting Master Wu, and the next day's visit to Stonehenge. "Karl talked with the curator of Stonehenge and got permission to explore, and possibly dig in certain areas," said Emily, holding her cup with both hands. "He said the curator had acknowledged instructions from higher up to allow us to do whatever was needed as long as none of the large stones were disturbed."

"I am always amazed at how easy Karl gets permission," said Greg. "I wonder if The Council has anything to do with the miraculous opening of ordinarily closed doors to sacred sites?" Emily smiled and raised her eyebrows.

Later, while they rested in their room, Greg's satellite phone chirped. "Yes, this is Greg Frostburg; I have been anxiously awaiting your call. Yes, we have much to discuss. Okay, good. We will meet you at the restaurant in an hour." Greg clicked the phone off and felt a rush of adrenalin. "Master Wu is here. Our venture begins soon."

Emily and Greg waited at the entrance to the hotel restaurant. A short, sturdy man with white hair and beard to match approached them. Greg smiled, and turned toward Emily. "This must be

Master Wu; his garb and demeanor remind me of characters I've seen in Kung Fu movies."

The man smiled and bowed when Greg introduced Emily and himself. They took a table in a quiet alcove. Once seated, they chatted about Emily and Greg's trip and the Master's interesting life, while they awaited their order. "I teach Kung Fu to future teachers with my son at his school in London." The Chinese man had grown up in a martial arts family, and learned the art of self-defense like an American child learns arithmetic.

After eating some very satisfying British food, the three left the restaurant and rambled along the road, discussing the Mission. "I love the beautiful countryside, and so many stones laying everywhere," Emily said.

Wu pulled a very unusual stone from his pocket and handed it to her. "I find this on way to Stonehenge while I travel here," Master Wu said. "I stop at pub to visit WC (toilet) and find this while I walk outside eating my crisps."

Emily turned the stone over examining the markings engraved on both sides. "This might have some connection with our quest. The marks look ancient. At least from what little I know of ancient communication." She handed it to Greg. "What do you think?"

Greg inspected the stone. "How could a stone like this not be noticed earlier? It seems strange that you just happened to find it."

The man shrugged. "Maybe we are guided."

"Yeah, maybe so." Greg held the stone up toward the sun. "I guess from a distance it might not be noticed. But with the many people and explorations that have occurred in that area, it just seems strange no one would have found it." He returned it to Master Wu. "Let's find someone who knows what these figures mean."

The Kung Fu Master nodded. They all drove to a nearby college and asked to speak to someone who could help them identify the stone and its engraving.

"That would be Professor Sanders." The woman at the information desk said. "His office is on the second floor, number 206." They thanked the woman and climbed the stairs.

After knocking on the office door, a man's strong voice said, "Come in."

The older man with a ruddy face and square-framed glasses turned in his sturdy chair. "Yes, I am Professor Sanders, how may I help you."

Emily explained their need to identify the engravings on the stone.

The Professor examined the stone. "Where did you find this?"

"At pub car park near Stonehenge." said Master Wu.

"This is quite a find," the Professor said in a reserved British accent. "It is probably 500 years old." He pulled a book from his library, and then placed it beside the stone. After a few minutes, he looked up. "The language is Celtic. It roughly reads: 'riches from above go below, stone by stone.' Since you found it near Stonehenge, it could have something to do with that ancient structure. I am surprised that some scientist did not find it sooner. Even scientists visit pubs." He smiled, and then handed the stone to the Chinese master. "Good luck." They thanked him and left.

As he opened the car door, Master Wu said, "Maybe symbols mean my Stone is 'riches' we look for. Maybe find above ground, and take below ground for Activation." He fastened his seat belt, and turned the stone over repeatedly in his hand. 'Stone by stone, puzzling."

Emily turned toward Master Wu. "Wow that is a wonderful translation of what it might mean to us. It sounds like someone guiding us to the Stone."

"I didn't mention this before, but The Council indicated that the Stone might not be at Stonehenge, but somewhere nearby and ..." Greg slowed the car and pulled to the side of the road, studying Salisbury Cathedral about a kilometer away.

Emily stared at Greg. "What are you doing?"

"I just got a vision about that spire. What if the 'above' means way above, like up in that 400 foot spire that's over 1000 feet above the ground?" Greg pointed to the large building.

The Chinese Master studied the cathedral, then the stone, then the cathedral again. "You maybe have a point. Makes more sense. We go." He smiled.

Emily smiled. "This is getting exciting. A couple of hours ago we didn't have a clue where we would start. Now look what you guys have come up with."

They returned to their hotel. Over their evening meal, they discussed Salisbury Cathedral.

"When I was resting earlier, I wondered if that building is old enough to have been used to hide a Stone?" Greg mused.

Wu put his chopsticks down. "That building is over 700 years old. I read pamphlet about the history years ago when I visit."

"Well, then I guess it is old enough." Emily stirred her tea "First test passed." She smiled at Greg.

Greg nodded. "Then the second 'test' as you call it, is getting permission to search the tower. Karl got permission to move beyond the barriers at Stonehenge to do some archeological work, but we had not thought about the cathedral."

"Not to worry. I know person there," the Kung Fu Master said.

Emily sat back with her tea cup cradled in her hands. "Okay, we are in the tower. What next?"

"I guess it will be like any other search we have done," Greg said. "We use our intuition, keep a sharp eye out for clues, and be very diligent."

They finished their meal, and then remained at the table wrapping up their plans for the next day, enjoying sherry trifle for desert.

The next morning, Greg loaded the rental car with his 'exploring' tools purchased at a DIY store in Salisbury, and the three adventurers headed toward Salisbury Cathedral.

When they arrived, Emily and Greg followed Master Wu to the western entry, where he visited an office and asked for an old acquaintance. After some discussion, the man returned.

He pointed up. "Ed in the tower. We can meet him there." They then found a door and climbed two flights of old, wooden stairs affixed to the stone tower's sides. Master Wu turned toward a room, and approached a man sitting behind a large desk. After a brief greeting, Ed asked Greg to explain their purpose for needing tower access. Greg used his archeological story for exploring Stonehenge and told the man that a possible clue to what he sought at the circle might be hidden in the tower.

"You want to poke around in a 500 year old structure affixed to the most magnificent cathedral in all of Britain to find an artifact connected to Stonehenge?" Ed gave Greg a puzzled look.

Greg nodded. "Well, yes. I know it may seem like a strange request, but your friend, Master Wu, can attest to its importance." He turned toward Wu.

The caretaker asked, "Is this true, my friend?"

"Yes, it is true." Master Wu smiled. "This man too technical. But age old story of ancestors hiding things to keep them away from the government, you already know, yes?"

The caretaker smiled. "You are so right. Seems unlikely, but maybe it is so. Okay, I give you charge of these two Americans. Make sure they don't break anything." He let out a short chuckle. "You have until closing time at five tonight. Check with me before your leave."

They left and then climbed the stairs.

"Not long we find Stone," the Master said.

"Yeah," came the disgruntled response from the tired traveler. "I thought the afternoon would be exploratory, and the main search for the Stone would be tomorrow, but now . . . I feel like I may not be able to stay alert." Greg held up a thermos. "But I brought some strong English coffee and determination with me." They stopped at the first stage of the tower, added in the 13th century, and looked outside.

Greg said to no one in particular, "Now where would an adept hide a Stone 400 years ago, knowing it had to remain hidden for perhaps hundreds of years. He would have put it in a place that wouldn't be disturbed by reconstruction and remain unaffected by weather."

"And not found by someone snooping around the interior." Emily studied the area.

They poked around the walls, ceiling and floor but found nothing that looked promising. Convinced this section contained no Stone, they moved upward to the next tower segment. Several areas contained loose stones and pockets where something could hide, but their detailed and exhaustive explorations led only to frustration for Greg. After two hours of fruitless searching, he just wanted the day to end so he could go back to the hotel and sleep.

Hopefully looking anywhere that might contain a clue, Emily stepped out onto a narrow porch-like area surrounding that part of the tower and stopped a moment to enjoy the view. She gazed out over the countryside and the cathedral's structure, which looked very different from this viewpoint. The added tower and spire gave the whole complex an authoritative and sacred air, especially with the afternoon sun reflecting from its metal garnishes. The outside part of the tower contained many decorative figures and niches — possible places to hide a Stone. Emily marveled at the workmanship carved into each wall, every stairwell, and splashed across the ceilings. The cathedral represented a masterpiece of not only spiritual expression, but artistry and creativity as well.

"Greg, Master Wu. We need to search out here, I think." Emily swept her hand around the balcony.

Greg raised his eyebrows. "Why? Did you see something or get a vision?"

"Well, maybe." Emily showed them the niches and other decorative areas that could hide something like a Stone.

"Okay, let's do it then." Greg set his bag of 'digging' tools on the floor.

Wu inspected one corner of the decorative balcony, Greg scrutinized another, and Emily checked near the top. They worked around the square structure, each proceeding in opposite directions. Halfway around his part of the search, Greg discovered an intriguing anomaly. A part of the stone railing near the floor contained a figure unlike any of the others. Its face's shape took on a stern look; all the others were cheery. He didn't think it even fit the period in which the tower was built, due to the way its arms were raised.

"Master Wu, what do you think of this?" Greg said.

Wu examined the figure. "Look like 17th century. See in museum."

"If that's so," Greg said, rubbing his hand over the piece, "then maybe our adept put it there."

"Hmmm, maybe." The Chinese man stepped back and studied the overall rail structure.

Emily joined the two and ran her fingers over the area. "Yes it does feel different."

Agreeing it warranted further examination, they focused on whether the piece was meant to be removed from its base or there was a way inside of it. Greg removed a large magnifying glass from his pack and examined each part of the figure. In what resembled a hand, he noticed a line or a crack between the 'hand' and a ball it held. He put his thumb and forefinger around the ball and twisted it. The piece of stone moved. He turned it more and it came off the carving. He held it in his hand and showed it to Master Wu and Emily.

Emily gasped. "My god I hope you didn't break it."

"No, look I can return it." He put the ball back and turned it so it was once again attached to the hand.

With Emily satisfied, he pulled it off again, and they scrutinized the 'ball' from every angle through the magnifier, but found nothing unusual. Greg got ready to return it to the figure, when Wu stopped him.

"Ah," he said sliding his finger over the bared area of the figure. "Sign."

"What?" Greg used the magnifier to inspect the smooth area. It bore a similar marking to one of those on the stone Master Wu had found near Stonehenge.

Emily glanced at Master Wu who pointed up. "It's a clue to show us where to search next I guess."

"Yes, clue." The Kung Fu master reached the doorway and poked his head inside, then looked up. "In the spire."

Before Greg returned the piece to the corner, Emily studied the ball intently and saw that the marking indeed resembled a spire. They followed Wu inside. The Kung Fu Master stood on the first rung of a ladder-like access to the spire.

Of course, Greg thought, what better place to hide something? He watched the agile man climb to a trapdoor and disappear through it.

Soon afterwards, Wu's head poked though the opening. "Someone come up. Hold light?"

Greg climbed to the opening. Master Wu handed him the light and pointed to an area of the spire he wanted to explore. Emily waited at the bottom ready to provide whatever help was needed.

The inside of the spire contained scaffolding used to maintain its integrity over the years. Greg lit the spire watching the shadows made by the scaffold dance around the ceiling. He knew that if climbing 'way up' into the spire's interior were necessary, Master Wu would have plenty of support. He brought the light back to the original area, and Master Wu climbed onto the scaffold. Greg then handed the light to him and climbed back down to get his own. He met Emily at the bottom.

"You want to take a peek up there or explore some?" Greg said.

Emily stared up at the hole. "That might be fun." She took the light, climbed the ladder, and poked her head through the opening. "Never saw the inside of a spire before. Looks better on the outside; smells better too. There is both a smell of dust and a musty odor up here. Since it is a closed area I would guess not much dampness gets in here; still, we are in England aren't we? Yuck, I could do without the cobwebs too." She smiled. Emily explored the foundation of the spire, while Master Wu investigated the area above her.

After 30 minutes, Emily called down to Greg. "Why don't you come on up here? It will go faster if we all look around this interesting place."

Greg climbed to the tower and joined Emily. "What have you checked?"

She pointed to a rafter just above them. "Just the area from here to there."

Greg put his hand on the rafter. "Okay, I'll go up there just below where Master Wu is and search that area. You can continue just below us if you want." Emily nodded. He climbed half-way up the spire using the light Emily had used. The light not only lit the area Greg explored, but also the area below helping Emily see better as well.

They all kept at it for another hour. There seemed to be plenty of places to hide something the size of a Stone, but none yielded the treasure. Finally, Master Wu called out, "I discover most interesting place." He had discovered a set of bricks that seemed unique and stuck out from the rest a bit.

Greg estimated the man to be 30 feet above him. He heard some scraping sounds, evidently from the man's small pick digging into the mortar around the bricks. Greg climbed to where Master Wu worked on the bricks that looked as though they had been added to the original. Greg scratched his head. "They were probably never noticed by workmen over the years, since you really needed to be looking for something in this area to notice." He helped the man remove one brick, then another, from some kind of metal plate and mortar. Then the Master leaned forward and grabbed something. Greg shone his light on the object

"Ah, most genius," said Master Wu.

Emily yelled to the men. "What's happening up there?"

"He has found a metal box hidden beneath the metal shield he removed from behind some bricks and mortar."

Wu searched for a way to open it. Greg heard something click. Then, the whole spire lit up, like someone had turned on a flood-light. Greg needed no explanation; the man had found the Stone.

Forty feet below the two men, Emily smiled. "Way to go Master Wu. Our first step has been found. Yes!"

The Kung Fu Master turned toward Greg. "Hold this please." He closed, and then handed the metal box to Greg. "I look more in hole." He turned and scraped more mortar out of the crevice. Greg could see him reaching into the hole. "Ah yes, beautiful." He turned toward Greg. "One more item." He handed it to Greg. He had found another object in the crevice, evidently to use in the ceremony. It looked like a piece of wooden tapestry. He turned back. "I will finish job." He carefully set the two bricks back in the hole. Since the metal box was missing, they fit into the hole snugly. The man pushed some cloth from a handkerchief around the bricks to assure their tightness.

The Master turned towards Greg, and pulled a sack from a pocket and held it out. Greg carefully placed the two items in the sack. The man tied the top, and then wrapped a rope around his waist. He then bound the bag to the rope. "Ready."

Greg took the cue and held his light so the man could descend without having to hold his own, allowing him to care for the precious items in the bag. Then Greg climbed down to where Emily and Master Wu talked. "We ready to take this baby home?" Greg said.

They climbed down to the floor of the tower. Emily hugged Wu and then Greg. "I am so excited. We are halfway there."

Greg smiled and returned Emily's hug, and then hugged the Master.

Making sure everything was back in place, they descended the tower. After thanking the caretaker for letting them explore, they made their way to the car as the sun drifted near the horizon.

When they closed the doors, Emily could feel dynamic energy coming from the Stone – like a swirling wind blowing against and around her body. Wu opened the box fully so they could all see the Red Stone. It displayed a mixture of reds and pinks with an oval shape. The Stone fit easily in Master Wu's palm, and Greg figured it to be about two inches in length and one inch in width.

"Awesome, huh?" The Master said.

Greg smiled. "Yes, indeed. Awesome it is."

While driving back to the hotel, Wu opened the box several times and admired the treasure. Each time, Emily not only saw the reddish-pink light from the box, which illuminated the car, but felt energy like none she had ever experienced. "Oh, I feel so empowered and more energized. It doesn't necessarily feel more powerful than the other Stones' energy I had felt during the first Mission, but maybe its vibration makes me sense it differently."

Wu also examined the object he had taken from the hole — it looked like lace, or a tapestry, although thicker but was actually made of wood. The six-inch piece looked almost white, perhaps bleached by the sun before the adept hid it in the tower. When they arrived at the hotel, each went to their room briefly, and then met for their evening meal.

"It's been our experience, so far," Emily said, "that the Stone will communicate with you. It's important for this to happen so we can find the Activation site."

The Kung Fu Master put his chopsticks down and smiled. "It talked to me in car. Also when I wash. Like a friend."

10

STONEHENGE CAR PARK

Kent Sourtaou paced in front of the rental car, his long, muscular arms swinging back and forth. *Where are those people? That pipsqueak has not shown his scrawny face all day.* He and two other men had sat in their car since early morning waiting for Greg and Emily. Tour buses and personal vehicles had come and gone without their targets. It was getting boring and frustrating, especially for him.

Kent poked his head into the open car window. "Going over there one more time and take a look." The other men nodded.

He strolled over to the rope that separated the huge stones from the public, scrutinized the area for guards, and stepped over the rope. Kent wandered amongst the gigantic stones, to make sure he had not missed his enemies sneaking about. He was amazed at the stones' size. *Wonder why people come here? Just to see big stones?* He leaned against one stone and lit a cigarette. While there, he felt something strange, at least to him. It seemed like a gentle breeze blowing against his back. He immediately withdrew from the stone. "What the hell?" *Ain't no wind blowing. Weird.* He made his way back to the car.

Kent dialed Fitzburg's number on his cell phone, but noticed there was no service in the area. He opened the car door. "We need to call Fitzburg. My cell phone don't get no signal. We'll go back to the hotel."

They drove to the small hotel in Amesbury, only 5 km away, where Kent called Halmar Fitzburg. "Those guys have not shown up. We waited all day. What now?"

"What time is it there," Fitzburg asked.

Kent glanced at the clock hanging over the reception desk on the yellow wall. "1720," said Kent.

"They will not start anything this late," said Fitzburg. "Go back in the morning. They may not have gotten there yet. Be patient. They will show up."

Kent hung up the phone and reported his conversation with Fitzburg. "We have the rest of the day off. Let's get some beer."

The three men spent the rest of the evening eating a light meal, talking, and drinking beer. "Hey Kent where are you from," said Friedrick.

Kent leaned back in the dark wood chair. "I grew up in the Midwest of the U.S. Can't say I much liked it. I moved to New York when I was 22, hung out for a couple years, and then hitched a ride on a steamer for Europe. Been here ever since taking odd jobs as they came along. What about you, Chase?"

"Not much to tell." Chase smiled. "I was born and raised in Germany. Got in trouble with the law when I was young and been staying in trouble ever since." He and the others laughed.

Friedrick took a swig of beer. "I guess I am next. I grew up in Italy. Worked as a mechanic for a few years, then joined this gang that tried to take over two blocks of street near where Monsignor Terkenni's church was located. A couple of his priests were alarmed and worked with the gang members to straighten them out. Terkenni took a liking to me and asked me to join a secret group he had formed, and that is where I worked until we got raided."

They all grew quiet for a few minutes, considering each of their revelations.

Then Friedrick asked, "Where do you think those Satanists are holed up?"

Kent shook his head. "I don't know, but when we find them, they will wish they stayed home. We will make them pay for all the trouble they are causing."

11

STONEHENGE

The next morning, after discussing their plans for exploring Stonehenge over breakfast, Emily, Greg, and Master Wu drove to the ancient site. When the stone circle came into view, Greg felt awestruck by its beauty — not so much beauty as in a sunset, but in the geometric design and the spiritual integrity of its grandeur. "Wow, I came here years ago while attending a conference in London, but the site meant nothing more to me as a young engineer, than a ring of rocks put there by some ancient people. Now, its true meaning comes through to me; they were placed in such a way as to give cosmic information to the ancient builders. Stonehenge, like the many sacred places around the world, is built on the intersection of ley lines; those invisible, but measurable energy grids of the earth. Wow."

"Yes, I feel it too." Emily watched the large stones as they drove past them. "I became familiar with this wondrous circle of huge stones through the Discovery Channel years ago, but once it became the first site for Mission 2, I read and searched the Internet to learn as much as I could before making this trip."

Greg drove into the car park and pulled in near the security building. "Me too, I learned that Stonehenge was thought to be an ancient "clock" and observatory of the cosmos, and had served as a sacred place for ritual, celebration, and burial of the dead. And now we are going to explore it."

Emily and Greg visited the people in the security building and presented the papers they had to visit all areas of the site.

"This says you are on an archeological mission." The security chief glanced at them. "What activities will you engage in from this perspective?"

Emily grew serious. "We have been instructed by a group that wishes to remain anonymous, to investigate certain areas that may reveal previously undiscovered information. This is all I can say."

"Okay, it has a British Government seal of approval, so I will stamp mine as well. Good luck." He handed the papers to Emily.

Greg nodded. "Thank you."

They left the building, met Master Wu and strode passed some tour buses. When they turned into a crosswalk with thick shrubbery on either side, Greg felt as though someone was behind him. Just as he turned, Kent Sourtaou lunged at him from behind a bush. Greg ducked and stepped aside, grabbing Kent's shoulder. The man could not stop in time, and Greg steered his head into the side of a lamp post. Meanwhile, the other two men attacked Emily and Master Wu.

As her attacker reached for her shoulder, Emily ducked, turned, and shot her right foot into the man's groin. When he doubled over in pain, she brought her knee up into his face, followed by a kick to his stomach.

Master Wu's assailant didn't have a chance. The Kung Fu Master made quick work of him by blocking the attack, grabbed the man's arms, and brought him to the ground. Once on the ground, Wu put his foot on the man's throat, and then delivered a disabling blow to the man's groin and stomach.

Meanwhile, Kent recovered from his head hitting the metal pole, and regained his awareness. He groggily attempted to stand

and get up off the ground. As he did so, Greg yelled to Emily, "Go get the guards. Send for the police." She ran toward the security building yelling for help and two guards ran out to meet her. Meanwhile, Master Wu sent a disabling blow to Kent's spine and Greg kicked him in the groin. The man doubled over in pain as he reached out to grab Greg.

Emily showed up with two guards, who then alerted the police. Friedrick managed to crawl away from the activity, hid behind a tourist group, and then some buses. When Friedrick got to the car twenty minutes later, the police showed up. He ducked behind the vehicle, opened the passenger side, and hid.

Meanwhile, the guards handcuffed Kent and the other man, and all five of them waited in the security building for the police. A lot of questions were asked, but since Emily had already explained their presence, before the attack happened, the three of them were not charged. Kent, even with severe injuries, attempted to break away from the police, but Greg and Wu helped put the man into the police cruiser. After filling out a brief form, Greg and company were requested to appear downtown to complete the charges against the two men, and Friedrick when the police found him.

"Wow, I expected they would show up, but not this soon," said Greg.

Master Wu watched the police cruiser drive away. "So that is opposition Karl told me about. Not too bad."

Emily and Greg laughed. "They might have been if you were not with us," said Emily. "I don't think they were expecting a third Martial Artist when they arrived."

"Well, if I hadn't gotten the drop on Kent, it could have been a lot worse for me. He was within three feet of me when I turned and surprised him." Greg put his hand on the pole. This and Kent's momentum saved my butt."

Master Wu still hadn't gotten the "stone by stone" part of the puzzle worked out, but figured once they connected with the huge circle of Sarsen and Blue stones, they would. They had arrived at the end of a public tour, and as they strolled, once again, across the car park toward the Stonehenge site entry, Emily overheard a remark from a young girl talking to her father while they boarded the bus.

"Daddy," she said. "Remember the lady told us that Stonehenge might have been like a clock? I'll bet that stone there" — she pointed to it – "must be number one. Look at its shape and location in the circle."

Emily said, "Out of the mouths of babes. That's it, of course – start with number one and follow the others to the site."

"You are most brilliant, Emily." Master Wu smiled. "Mystery solved, yes?"

Gaining approval from one of the guards posted at the circle, the three explorers examined the "number one" monolith. On one side, they found a distinct marking: an arrow that pointed across the circle to another monolith, perhaps beyond it. They lined up the next stone, and moved towards it. Once there, Master Wu noted that beyond it two similar stones aligned perfectly with the first two. They got to the next boulder beyond the circle, and noticed two more aligned with it. By the time they got to the last boulder, Greg figured they had moved a hundred yards from the circle of monoliths.

"Look, the remnants of other large rocks spread out in either direction," Emily said. "Perhaps there was originally an outer circle, and these other rocks were its 'spokes.'"

They moved to an outer area beyond the circular mound that contained the large ring of stones. Emily pointed. "Look near the outer fence at that peculiar-looking stone. It may be what we are looking for." They hurried to the place she had indicated.

"This looks like the last one," Greg said. "I see no stones beyond or near this one."

They studied it carefully. It had no distinct markings, but when Master Wu stood back a few feet he noticed a peculiar shape to it. "Look, stone points down."

Emily and Greg backed away from the large rock. "I see what you mean," said Emily. "This one is larger at the top making it look like an indicator *pointing down*."

"Yes," said Greg. "If the weather had caused the odd shape, the stone would have worn from the top downward."

"Now all we have to figure out is what 'down' means." Emily ran her hand along the boulder.

They spent the next hour trying to move the stone, moved around it, and searched everywhere for the next step. Then, Emily ran her fingers along what looked like the foundation of the stone. It resembled a rope.

"What did you just do?" Greg asked.

Emily looked up. "I just ran my fingers across this bump along the bottom."

"Do it again." Greg pointed to a grassy place about ten feet away. "I thought I saw a mist over there like when I was in Hawaii searching for the first Stone."

Master Wu strolled towards them just as she ran her fingers over the spot, and then suddenly disappeared.

"Oh my god; Master Wu." Emily cried out. "Where are you?"

Greg ran over to where the man had stepped. "When you did that again I saw the mist again. Then Master Wu stepped into it. I think we have found a portal."

Emily moved to where Greg stood. "If we have, how do all three of us get through it, and how do we get back out?"

"I don't know, but one of us has to go in there with a light." Greg grabbed a light from his bag. "Touch it, or whatever you did, again. I'll need this light to find a way back." She knelt down, repeated her action and Greg disappeared.

Greg felt like he had fallen through a cloud. He lit the light and found he stood next to a dirt wall.

"Ah, I am glad you join me," came the voice of Master Wu.

Greg got up and turned toward the voice. The man stood a few feet away.

"How did you get here?" The man said.

Greg explained Emily touching the stone. "What we need to find out now is how to get back."

Wu swept his hand across a dirt wall. "I poke about in here but find no return. Now we have light."

They searched the dirt wall behind them.

"Look, stones in the walls and over there are ... wait a minute. It's a huge circle; we are under Stonehenge." Greg exclaimed.

The Kung Fu master took a deep breath. "Yes, we go back, gather what I need."

"Most likely, we will open the portal in a similar way as did Emily." Greg searched for a stone like the one Emily touched. "Over there, maybe that one will do the trick." He and Wu made their way to the stone.

Master Wu knelt and then laughed. "Did she touch this piece here?"

"Yes, she ran her fingers over it." Greg said.

Wu did the same and the two of them were surrounded by a mist, and then transported to the grassy place from which they had entered the portal.

"Greg, Master Wu! I crossed my fingers you would find a way back." She hugged them.

Greg explained what they had found. "We need only to collect whatever Master Wu needs to do the Activation and come back before sunset. Let's get something to eat."

When Emily explained to the guard at the car park that they needed to leave for awhile, and would return a couple of hour before dark to complete their work, he smiled. "It is the Equinox. The gates will remain open past dark for the many fans that gather on such occasions."

"It may get crowded when we return," Emily said as she got into the car. "We may have to be more watchful this evening."

Master Wu smiled. "This good. It will help Activation."

They drove to town, had some lunch, and discussed their steps once they returned to Stonehenge. "Disappearing and then reappearing may be tougher to hide with many people there." Greg wrinkled his brow. "But I guess once the Activation is complete, it won't matter. We just can't let anyone watch our activities, lest they try it too."

"We have about a 20 second window to get into the portal spot." Emily ate some chips. "We cannot let anyone get near it once I set the opening. That may be our biggest challenge."

They finished their meal and agreed on details of how they would approach the spot, touch the stone, and get into the portal. The three explorers gathered some water and headed back to Stonehenge.

When they arrived at the car park, the number of vehicles had more than doubled since they had left. They let the guard know of their return and headed toward the 'portal stone'.

While there were a lot of people at the Stonehenge circular mound, they had not spilled over onto the grassy area where the three needed to stand. Just after sunset and the Activation, the possibility of crowds expanding into the area increased.

"Are we ready?" Emily kneeled near the stone. The other two stood in the grassy area and nodded. She touched the stone in the unique way she had before, joined them, and waited. A few seconds later they found themselves in the dark. They lit their lights and quizzically explored the huge 'core' beneath Stonehenge.

An increase in energy filled the entire cavern – like the vibration from a swarm of bees. "Do you feel the energy here?" Emily put out her hands.

"Yes plenty enough. Under the circle of stones above." Master Wu pointed above his head. He busied himself exploring the cavern, touching outcrops of rocks and ledges, searching for just the right one.

Greg watched Wu making preparations and marveled at their discovery. "As always, we find such amazing places, but cannot tell someone about it."

"Yeah, to do that would jeopardize the Mission." Emily said.

Master Wu turned toward the center. When he did, his light uncovered a group of large, flat rocks. The grouping resembled a table in the center of eight stools. Wu sat on one of the 'stools' and unloaded his pouch onto the 'table'. He took out the Red Stone and placed it in the center of the almost perfectly round rock that now served as an altar for the Activation ceremony. Once set there, its radiance increased until the whole cavern glowed in a reddish-white light. Master Wu gazed at the Red Stone, fully focused and immersed in its light.

"He must be getting direction for the ceremony," Emily whispered. She stood near the group of rocks watching. "The energy coming from the Red Stone feels like trying to push two magnets of the same polarity against each other."

The Kung Fu Master glanced up at them and said that he would repeat what he was doing in English so they could follow him. Emily nodded.

Master Wu chanted for a few minutes in his native language, which Greg understood only a part of. But "chi," meaning 'life-force' or energy, and some other words caught his attention. Near the end of Wu's chant, a tall, hazy figure appeared above the Red Stone. Its brilliant, white radiance mixed with the Red Stone's, caused a mist-like haze of white light tinged with red to encompass the altar, stools and Master Wu. The apparition spoke in a firm, yet soft male voice.

"Welcome to the sacred ceremony that you have released me to direct. I am Mahaia. I will guide you to the completion of this Stone's Activation. Kindly place the tapestry under the Red Stone, then sprinkle some of the water you collected over both."

The Chinese Master complied and stepped back from the altar. A tiny violet glow appeared at the base of the Red Stone and spread out across the tapestry. As it did, the tapestry changed into a white, lace-like web that climbed around the Red Stone, completely enclosing it. Emily thought it resembled a wedding cake ornament: one with a lace canopy over the bride and groom.

A mixture of colors emerged from the structure and music came from within. It sounded like a thousand melodious voices in a choir, backed by hundreds of flute-like instruments. Mahaia chanted with the music and asked that they join him.

Greg had not heard such a chant in all the groups he had been a part of over the years. It combined the vibrational characteristic of most chants with lilting musical tones that sent ripples of loving energy up and down his spine. Master Wu experienced similar feelings, and his tears flowed shamelessly. The lights dimmed and music faded until only a glimmer remained.

Mahaia spoke again. "It is indeed beautiful, my friends. Thank you for reaching into my realm with me. Now, once again; sprinkle a few drops of water on the structure."

As Master Wu did so, the structure expanded from beneath the Stone with 'spokes' spreading in all directions. Emily counted twelve in all and each spoke's color was red with a rainbow-colored ball at its tip. The balls vibrated, each with a different tone, sending sound into every crevice of the cavern. This time a dance-like melody played and all four of them danced in harmony with it. The whole room vibrated, first in alignment with the music, then steadier and louder. The vibration resembled a low-pitched hum and felt like a person would when standing on a vibrating platform.

While dancing, Emily noticed that the Red Stone and the structure surrounding it changed color in sync with the vibrations in the cavern. A different color flowed through each 'spoke' in harmony with the sounds. Then the colors and music faded as it did before. All of this lasted for ten minutes, Greg guessed, as he stopped moving. Mahaia spoke again. This time a red light came from above and focused on the Stone.

"This Red Stone exemplifies the Life-force that flows through you, and calls the Red Cosmic Ray that symbolizes life, strength, power and vitality. These words may seem to imply that a great, powerful being is forceful and physically strong, yet that is only part of it and may not even be so. Power comes from within, and may be used in a gentle, loving way in any situation, and is far more effective than force. There are times when one or the other, or both, are needed. Mastering the body allows it to be used as a tool for Spirit. The Life-force anchors the body in Spirit, so that the soul using that body focuses on service as a way of life.

Going within is the key, allowing a person to identify with the spiritual, rather than having the energy flow outward to the sensory world. You are in the world, not of it, and must identify that which is 'worldly' in nature and apart from your inner being. There is a balance. You would not be here if you were not to partake of the world in some way, but you alone can find this way and it is found from within. The 'within' turned outward moves you into the loving, compassionate Being you truly are, and onward to serve others. Self-knowledge and introspection is heightened by using the Red Ray during meditation and allows you to remove obstacles to happiness, peace and Unconditional Love."

Mahaia shifted his tone slightly. The gentle voice took on a sterner note, and even the colors moving around the room became brighter and moved faster.

"The director of the Life-force in the human body is the ego, or life-ego. It presides over the life and generative function of the body, and is the center of activity and sensation. The ego must attend to three main factors of consciousness: intelligence, life, and substance. The flow of energy through the physical body is sensed in the spiritual body, but it is the ego that sends this life-stream to every faculty. Sensation is the connecting link between the quick-moving spiritual vibrations and the slow, heavy vibrations of the physical. It is a mental quality and depends on your spiritual characteristic for its full satisfaction.

The ego, however, can never be a master, but must yield to you, the spiritual director of the physical actions and thoughts it portrays. The ego must be an ally, not an enemy to be eliminated, so that a balance is established. You are in a physical body for a reason, and the ego directs it through your will, and no other."

Mahaia gently touched the top of Master Wu's head, like a king would have with a sword when knighting someone. He then reached out and touched Emily's and Greg's heads in the same manner. Greg felt a warm tingling, then a chill pass through his body when Mahaia touched his head. "You are knights of this world, bringing your talents to help the people here discover their own greatness. Before I leave you, I have a message for Emily."

Emily took a step toward Mahaia, but then she seemed to hear a voice in her mind. The spiritual being spoke to Emily telepathically and revealed the location of the next site. "You are to keep this knowledge secret and reveal it only to those who need to know."

Mahaia then bowed. "Bless you. You may leave. The two stones that opened the portal will cease to function once you are on the surface again. It is finished." With that sentence, the cavern vibrated and filled with energy such that Emily found it difficult to stand. Then amazingly the stone configuration sank into the flat rock, while Mahaia hung over it like a guardian.

Wu and the other two knelt in reverence to the Red Stone's light that now came from rock's top. Emily made her way to the 'portal stone' and ran her fingers along the 'bump' at the bottom. Instantly, the three were back on the surface amongst a crowd gathered around the circle of Stonehenge. Fortunately, they appeared without anyone noticing, since most were mesmerized by the full moon and Equinox energy.

Strolling toward the large stone circle and the exit gate, Emily could feel a slight vibration, which increased somewhat when they passed near the center. They apprised the guards that they had finished, and then got into their car. None of them spoke until they were driving back to the hotel.

Master Wu smiled. "Awesome." And patted Greg's shoulder.

Smiling, Greg said. "I am almost speechless right now, but your word is right on."

"Wow, indeed it is." Emily spread her arms out against the seat.

"We need to watch ourselves for the rest of this trip even though the Activation is complete." Greg glanced in the mirror at Master Wu, while he spoke. "I just hope when you return to your normal lifestyle that those men we fought forget about your involvement with the Mission."

"My pleasure to serve planet. Mission worth it. I be okay." Master Wu sunk down in his seat, folded his arms and smiled. "When I go back, see son, he know I do awesome thing."

Greg peered in the mirror again while pulling away from the curb. "Still, I feel them looking over my shoulder; even now."

They drove the rest of the way to the hotel, silent once again, as the last rays of the sun disappeared. Master Wu went to his room, while Emily and Greg headed for theirs. Once inside Greg glanced at Emily. "Well?"

"Well, what?" Emily gave him a blank look.

Greg put his hands on his hips. "You know 'what'; the 'message' Mahaia gave you."

"Oh, that?" She smiled. "It is the location of the next site. But I cannot tell you here." She tore off a piece of paper from a pad and placed it on the glass-covered top of the lamp table. She wrote the name of the site and the secrecy Mahaia had mentioned. She then showed it to Greg. It had the name "Altai Mountains, Russia" on it.

"Wow. I see. Okay I understand." He then lit the paper with a match, put it in an ashtray until it burned, and then flushed the ashes down the toilet. They then left and met Master Wu in the dining room.

They all were cheery and talkative when they met for dinner. Having used the 'Life-Force' all his life through martial arts, calling it 'chi', he knew its potential and expression through him. He felt honored being chosen to perform "such an honorable mission."

"The Mission is honored by you, Master Wu, as am I," Emily said. "We accomplished a monumental task this day, my friend, and you made it possible. Our opponents have been kept at bay for now, thanks to you."

Emily touched her heart. "On another note, we as martial artists have all practiced with our Life-Force in many ways, especially you Master Wu, but I personally feel the energy moving through me even more today due to the activation."

"Yes, I feel it too," said Greg, "but when it comes to my ego guiding that Force it throws me off a bit. I believe the Life-Force comes from deep within my being or heart. That is where I find my range of gentle to powerful during my meditations as well as my Kung Fu."

The next morning, on their way to London, Emily and Greg stopped at the police station and filled out the necessary forms.

The men who attacked Greg and the others would be held for ten days, so that Emily and Greg could safely leave the country. After that, Greg wondered what those men would do next.

12

SEDONA, AZ

Karl Josephon studied the email, its content disturbing. He sat back heavily in the sturdy chair with a sigh. *It's started already. The first day they set foot on a new sacred place seeking a Stone or its Activation site, Fitzburg and his cronies were there. Terkenni's exit hadn't stopped a thing.*

He looked up from the computer and glimpsed a hawk gliding by the open window. "Well, one thing we discovered my friend," he followed the hawk as if in conversation, "is that we now have the next site." Karl stood and stretched. "Time for lunch." He busied himself in the kitchen and was about to drink some cinnamon tea, when the doorbell rang.

Karl opened the door to a radiant looking woman with long black hair and crystal-blue eyes. "May I help you?"

"You may indeed, Mr. Josephon. My name is Christina Kylingten. I have been following the articles your company has been writing for *Sedona Magazine*; one of them saved my life." She paused and then took a deep breath. "I would like to interview you and the other members of your company for the *Sedona Red Rock News*. Can we set up a time for me to do that?"

Karl invited her into the spacious living room and offered her a cup of tea. Sitting across from her he said, "My colleagues are currently out of the country, and I cannot speak for them regarding an interview, but I am willing to participate for a short period. I am currently running the classes for Ancient Wisdom Seminars here in Sedona, and coordinating the schedule for our classrooms in two other countries. If an interview with me alone would work for you, I have some time this afternoon and next week. Oh, and call me Karl."

She leaned forward and drank some of the cinnamon tea. "Thank you, Karl. While I would like to interview all of you at once, one at a time will do. Next week will work nicely." They chatted awhile longer, and then she left.

Karl watched her leave and shook his head. *Wonder where that came from? Are we getting that popular?* He ate lunch, and then gathered some books, and headed to the classroom on the edge of town. It sat amongst some stores in a strip mall and looked out at Cathedral Rock to the south. He unlocked the door and sat in one of the desks for awhile, getting a feel for the environment a student might have. "Well, Karl you are on tomorrow. Make it count."

The next morning, Karl welcomed the new students. Fifteen showed up and, surprisingly, eight were men. He pulled away the empty chairs and stacked them in a corner. He felt empty chairs decreased the energy of the room. "You have probably figured out that I am not Emily Benson as it says on your introduction sheet. She is off collecting information to make our classes even better. My name is Karl Josephon, and I will be entertaining you this week." The class responded with laughter and cheers. Karl figured that he had a fairly diverse group, both in experience and age, since about half looked to be in their late twenties and early thirties, and the rest in their fifties and beyond.

"This is the first class in a series of five. Each one builds on the other. You can see in your handout that they range from five days to three. The longer classes give you the time to assimilate what will seem like new ideas in the first two classes, ask questions, and then discuss the process. The last two classes are only three days, but with a day break in between each one. This gives you a whole day to contemplate what you learned from the class. That's the outline. If there are no questions, let's get started."

Karl paused a moment, answered a couple of questions about the class synopses, and then continued. "From the time we are children through adulthood we are told how and what to do by just about everyone in our lives. It seems that other people have all the answers, and we are like robots taught to do certain things specific ways in order to coexist in society. We store that information in our subconscious minds as *beliefs*, just as a computer would store info on its hard drive."

He paused a moment, and then continued. "Along the way, we are also told to go to college, earn a degree and make big bucks because of it. This education and the money earned will supposedly make us happy. We will fulfill the 'American Dream' of a big house in the country, marry the perfect mate, and have a fantastic family. All because we followed what we were told. Well, I am here to tell you that we have been led astray." Some shook their heads in agreement, others stared at him blankly.

"How many of you think you live a happy life?" One hand went up. "Given the proper techniques and guidance, how many think you *could* live a happy life?" Several hands went up. Karl smiled. "If you follow the lessons in this course and participate in the exercises and activities, I guarantee your chances of making that come true is close to 100%." He swept his hand around the room and toward the one window and door. "You see, it is not about what is going on out there; or even in this classroom." He touched his heart "It's what is in here that counts. And that is what we will learn more about this week."

He strolled around the room checking body language to get a feel for how this statement came across. "Going back to what I said earlier about how we learn and store beliefs in our subconscious, those beliefs are what drive us to do what we do. But suppose we overwrite those beliefs like you would your hard drive, and install another program? Well that is what you are going to do this week."

Karl checked the room for hands, and then went on. He challenged them to tell him who they thought they were. "I am a baker," said one. "I am an engineer," said another. These kinds of identities came forth from those who were willing to answer. Then, a woman in the back of the room raised her hand. "I am a child of God."

Karl smiled. "That is the closest answer to the truth of who you are." The others wore puzzled looks. "We will explore the answer to this question when we come back from lunch. It will lead us into the happiness part." They left the building, some eating a snack at the picnic area, or gathering at a nearby restaurant. When they returned, Karl dove into the subject of identity.

"We have learned to identify ourselves with what we do at work, for a business, or profession. Early in life our name is who we think we are and we continue to add identities throughout our lifetime. But none of them is who we really are. Suppose each one of us is a powerful spiritual being who creates his or her own life?" He paused a moment, giving them a chance to contemplate this notion. "Yes, we are the creators of our every moment. We decide if the next moment will be wonderful or rotten. How? Let's get back to reprogramming the hard drive."

Karl leaned against the edge of the desk. "We have two aspects of our mind – the conscious and subconscious. The conscious mind is what guides us from an aware state; it is the 'driven' aspect of our mind. Whereas the subconscious, otherwise known as the unconscious, mind is the 'controlling' part of our mind. If you were to compare the two from a position of strength or power, the conscious aspect would be like an obedient recruit, and the unconscious like a muscular sergeant barking orders. You see, the subconscious is where our belief-system lies, and it is from our beliefs that we create our lives. Trouble is, we really don't know what is stored there."

He went on to explain the idea of Oneness and that we are each a unique aspect of the One, or what most call God. The rest of the afternoon, they discussed this concept from several different angles, in order for everyone to get a better idea of where their perspectives led them.

Most of the students left with the Oneness idea to contemplate. Some had great difficulty believing such a thing was possible. Karl felt that he had accomplished what he had planned for this class. While the amount of procedural work given the class did not amount to much, the vastness of the idea gave them plenty to consider.

After returning home, Karl prepared his evening meal and considered his next project. He needed to start compiling the list of possible countries where they could set up new classrooms and recruit teachers to serve them. It had been a tough job so far.

That evening, Karl chatted on the phone with Emily and Greg who were contemplating their next steps. Since they now had the geographic location of the next site to explore, they could travel there. But first, someone needed to determine the name and personal information of the next recipient. It didn't make sense for Karl to contact The Council, get the name and info for the next Recipient, and then call Emily and Greg.

They decided that Emily would make these calls since she would have contacted the Recipient after receiving the info from Karl anyway. Karl felt relieved. "Now I can focus on Ancient Wisdom Seminars and teaching classes," Karl said. "Since I know the contacts for providing you two with a legitimate story at each site, I will maintain that function."

"As it should be," said Emily. "The less you have to contact us, the less our phone conversations will be compromised."

After completing the call, Karl thought about The Cause and their continuing threat to everyone connected to their company. *We, no the world, have a lot riding on how each of us plays our part in completing this Mission.*

13

MOSCOW

A gray winter-like sky hung over the Antiquities Museum in Moscow. Nikitrina Sanstov, called "Niki" by her fellow workers, glanced out of the window behind her desk and let out a sigh. She got up and poured a cup of coffee from the pot near the desk of her friend, Rita. "I am growing weary of gray. I know winter weather is coming, but a day of sun occasionally would help my mood." Rita nodded in agreement.

The large office area was crammed with desks and a dozen workers. Niki had worked in the same drab room for seven years and yet enjoyed her work searching, cataloging, and going to sites to investigate claims of antiquities and artifacts. She felt like an archeologist while digging through the dirt and brushing off pottery and other pieces that might wind up in the museum. But she longed for the sunshine of Spain where she vacationed.

"Ну хорошо," said Niki. "Oh well. Vacation time will have to wait." She returned to her desk and continued her work. But even while she worked, Niki felt a longing. At first, she was not sure what it meant; it was not about vacation, but something deeper.

Later, on her way home, Niki rounded a corner of the busy street, and noticed a sign on the side of a building that she had not seen before. *The Altai Mountains. That is where Siria lives. Brr, even colder than here.* Siria was a Shaman that Niki had taken lessons from for the past year. While their communications had mostly been by phone, she knew her next visit to the Shaman was due soon.

Through her studies, Niki had obtained great knowledge of the ancient people in the area. That is how she had become interested in Shamanism, and studied books about the area's Shamanistic past. During her studies, she had met Siria and gained a great appreciation for the woman's work.

Once home, Niki remembered the feeling at work that she could not quite identify. *Siria, my work with her; this is what I am feeling. I will call her and ask that she lead me through a Shamanic journey.* Just as she picked up the phone, the doorbell rang. When she opened the door, she exclaimed, "Siria! I was just calling you. Are you real, or are you an image?"

Siria put out her arms, and then hugged Niki. "Yes, my dear Niki, I am real. But surely you knew that I am aware of your intentions." Siria smiled. "And here I am."

Niki gave the woman a startled look. "But . . ."

Siria laugh. "Just kidding with you. On my way home from a conference, something spoke to me about your next lesson. I knew I needed to visit and coach you through a journey."

After the two women had some coffee, they made preparations for the Shamanic journey. Siria asked, "On what do you want to focus?"

"My destiny."

"Let us begin then," the woman said.

Niki brought her drum and flute to the Shaman, and then sat on a bear rug she used for ceremonies. She felt the energy build differently than it had on other journeys, while Siria brought the drum beat to a shamanic rhythm. The energy increased much faster and more vividly than it had the other times. Niki fell into a deep trance and began experiencing a vision.

She was lying on a snow-covered mountainside watching the sunrise over a peak with two points. Near her left and right hips were white wolves, and a white leopard sat in front of her. The leopard moved across a small plateau and then down a slope, and she got up and followed. The two wolves followed her — one still at her side, the other slightly behind her.

The leopard led Niki through forests, across streams, and to a waterfall still flowing even with the freezing cold temperature. Then the leopard stopped and sat on the snow. She stood beside it and watched while a majestic Being surrounded with white light came from the waterfall. It held an object that glowed brighter than the sun. The leopard and wolves bowed, while the figure held the object in front of her heart.

The Being returned to the waterfall, and motioned for Niki to follow. She led Niki through the waterfall into a huge cave, lit with golden light. The wolves and the leopard followed, and stood outside of the cave entrance like guards. The figure then led Niki down a spiraling, golden staircase that ended in a gold and silver room filled with splendid jewels.

Suddenly Niki was outside looking through the waterfall at the setting sun. A swirling wind picked her up and she felt as one with the light, the sky and the cosmos. Then like a wisp of wind everything vanished and she came back into the room with Siria.

Niki told Siria about the vision. "What does it mean?"

"It is not for me to tell you." The Shaman put her hand on Niki's heart. "You must look inside yourself. There lies the answer. I feel you will know more soon." She got up. "I must go. We will meet again before long." They hugged and the Shaman left.

The next evening, while Niki ate supper, the phone rang. It was Emily calling to inform Niki about her task. Emily explained her role in the Mission, and that Niti's name was given to her by people called The Council. Niki would be the person who would find and activate a Wisdom Stone somewhere in the Altai Mountains; the Recipient.

"To Altai? Siria was right. She knew you would be calling me." She went on to tell Emily about her vision. "I will take some time off from work and let them know in the morning. It is time for my vacation anyway. I am ready to follow my vision."

14

ROME, ITALY
MUNICH, GERMANY

The streets were wet, the air cold and damp, as Kent and Friedrick scampered down Ave St. Filo in East Rome. "Why are we here?" Kent asked.

"Fitzburg says that if we can hole up in that place Terkenni used, we would have a headquarters." Friedrick put his hands in his pockets. "We look the place over and report to him what we find."

Kent shook his head. "But that is where Terkenni got caught. Seems dangerous to stay there."

Friedrick nodded. "Well that is what he wants."

They moved fast through the falling rain until they reached their destination. "Here it is." Friedrick pointed towards the red building.

They tried the door. When it would not open, they scurried around the building seeking other entries. Kent spotted the dumpster Isabel had used, and jumped up on it. "Looks abandoned. We would have ta' break in. What if somebody is watchin'?" Kent shook his head. "Too dangerous." He hopped down, and they circled the building, with the same results. Finding no *legal* entryway, they left.

An hour later, in a dimly lit corner of a small downtown bar, Halmar Fitzburg stood stiffly, his hands on his hips. "That is all you have to report?"

"Yes sir." Friedrick twitched as he spoke. "As you know that is the place where Monsignor Terkenni held a kidnapped hostage, and both the police and religious leaders raided it."

Halmar slid into a padded chair on one side of the table. "I see your point. Then we will make a headquarters elsewhere. It is time for me to return to Munich. We will work from there." He glanced at the others. "Agreed?" They all nodded.

Two days later, the same group of men sat together in a large room on the southern edge of Munich, Germany. Fitzburg had procured the use of a spare room in a military complex he once ran as commander in chief.

"Well now, this is more suitable for our status as guardians of the State." Halmar glanced around the table. "What do you say?"

Kent stood, and then took a few steps to a large, marble statue near the table. "We are near great figures." He touched the statue. "I say we are meant ta' be here."

Friedrick stood and held up a glass of wine. "To Commander Fitzburg and our new headquarters." The rest toasted Halmar, who joined them.

Fitzburg felt a radiance within while he drank, like he did when he led soldiers into battle. He smiled. "Now, we need to disperse and find those hellions." Fitzburg moved to a large, world map affixed to a wall. "We have found their next intended destination since leaving England. A group here works with spy satellites and other listening and locating equipment. They overheard a conversation between this Emily person and the guy in Sedona, Karl. They are headed for Biisk airport in Russia." He pointed to the area with a ruler. "I have sent three men to follow them. Meanwhile, we stand by and wait for our next move."

Halmar paced the wooden floor. "We have two other options to obtain information: the first, Karl in Sedona, and second, his girlfriend, Shannon in Madrid. Should we lose track of the two searchers again, we have to create fall back positions. Are you prepared?"

They all nodded.

"One way we can find them is to threaten Shannon McKinksley and see what we can accomplish with that move. Another way is to engage Karl Josephon in Sedona and question him. He is the only one that keeps track of where they are. When the time comes, you three," he pointed to two of the men who had been in Sedona earlier, and his 'right hand man' Gedof, second in charge, "are good at getting what we want from people. Agreed?"

They raised their arms and shouted "Yes!"

"The rest of us will make plans to threaten, and capture if necessary, Shannon McKinksley and how we will handle that situation should it arise. By God, we are ready to overthrow these enemies no matter what. Right?" He banged his fist on the table.

They all followed him loudly banging the table as well, and said in unison, "right!"

15

ALTAI MOUNTAINS, RUSSIA

mily and Greg moved through Russian customs in the Barnaul airport; their rendezvous point with Niki. She met them at noon and took them to a nearby restaurant to discuss their plans for getting to Biisk. It was a rendezvous point with Niti's friend, Sergi, their transportation to Siria's cabin in the Altai Mountains, in the southern part of West Siberia, near Mongolia.

"Besides equipment and clothing for the temperatures and snow we will encounter," Niki said, "you also may want to buy some climbing and camping equipment. We will stay in Siria's cabin at night, but that could change, and you will have it for emergencies. I am very excited about going back to the mountains, because I will be with Siria searching for this mysterious gem: my destiny. The snow does not beckon me as much as it used to, but I will get by."

"I, too, am exited about this trip. I've always wanted to visit Siberia and the Altai region." Emily put her hand on Niki's hand.

Greg enjoyed the Turkish espresso. "I was hoping to try this, but I had to sooth its bite with this great honey." He smiled, knowing that the women were immersed in an 'antiquities' conversation and didn't hear him. Niki's tall, blond and blue-eyed frame seemed typical of Russian women he had seen in movies. Her muscular body revealed athletic prowess that would prove invaluable during the next few days.

As morning arrived, they boarded their train for Biisk. The Siberian countryside looked even more picturesque than Greg had imagined. It reminded him of Vermont with its rolling hills and distant mountains covered with light snow. Many years had passed since he last traveled by train and it felt brand new in such a faraway place. This train showed signs of an older locomotive with modern updates.

Greg felt confident that Niki had done her homework, and made the appropriate contacts. She seemed intelligent, intuitive, and perceptive in terms of the journey on which they were about to embark. Niki sounded as if she had experienced many Siberian winters, even though she vacationed south of Russia.

They sat in silence and listened to clacking wheels hit rail joints. Greg felt peaceful and imagined a ball of love inside his head that expanded outward and moved downward into his heart, releasing heartfelt energy. The coach seemed like a carriage carrying a princess to her castle. They were her servants, aiding her travel to a magical land.

The jolt of the train stopping stirred Greg from his contemplation and brought him back to the awareness of a large seat under his stiff bottom. They grabbed their bags and headed for the station exit. Niki's friend, Sergi, who would be their new guide, met them outside, and helped pile their bags in the back of his vehicle. He stopped near the edge of Biisk at his favorite restaurant, where they ate another scrumptious Russian meal with Borsch, Kraniki for the two vegetarians, Greg and Emily, and pumpkin Oladi for dessert. Greg had watched people during their trip from Barnaul, and hadn't seen any suspects. But he knew they would most likely show up at some point.

A cold wind blew snow across the road as they climbed higher in their rugged mountain vehicle. They had visited two villages, stopping for a warm drink, and a light snack at one of them. During their meal, Emily had watched Sergi and listened to his tales about the Altai region and his adventures. His high cheekbones and brown skin reflected his Turkish and Mongolian heritage. Sergi knew the area well, and had years of experience as a guide. Emily felt safe and confident with him at the wheel.

Sergi stopped in front of a decorative cabin on the fringe of a little village. Its wooden construction and green shutters reminded Greg of a German "gingerbread" house, since many people of German decent had moved to this area during the WWII era. Poking through the semi-thatched and wood roof, a brick chimney puffed smoke into the mostly gray sky.

"We are here," Niki said, and opened the Jeep's door to a cold wind blowing through her long hair hanging from beneath a fur-rimmed cap.

They followed while a small woman with long, white hair emerged from the house. She and Niki hugged, and then Niki turned. "Emily, Greg this is my good friend Siria."

When Greg approached her, he seemed drawn into Siria's crystal-blue eyes. He felt as if he looked *through* them into another world. Then, after he hugged the woman and backed away, her eyes reflected *him*. He could not only see his body, but deeper within the person beyond the physical. Amazingly, he saw a powerful spiritual being, an etheric image, whose service to the world spoke for him. *Could this be who I truly am?* He refocused on Siria, who radiated a powerful and loving energy that made him feel welcome without speaking.

"I witnessed your Mission two moons ago through my daughter-to-be," Siria said, her voice strong yet soft. "You have power available to you, of which you do not know. It need only be called forth. Come, let us share hot soup in my dwelling." She turned and opened the door. Greg assumed the "daughter-to-be" reference had to do with Niki's instruction as a Shaman.

The room was warm, bright, and welcoming. Its muted brown, red and orange colors and furnishings painted a picture of austere elegance. Emily felt like she had traveled back through time to the 1800's as she surveyed the wooden table and chairs, the large fireplace and massive rug covering half the wooden floor. A fire crackled in one corner, enclosed by the stone fireplace that seemed to reach out into the room, calling them to its hearth. Pouring the hot soup into large cups, Siria passed them amongst the group. When all were served, she joined them near the fire.

"Oh, how marvelous," Emily said, as she lowered her spoon. "This is all vegetable isn't it?"

Siria smiled. "Why, yes my dear Emily. I am so happy that you like it."

"I love it!" Emily said. "I've never tasted a vegetable soup with such a rich taste. What's the broth made from? It's so unusual."

"It is based on a recipe that found its birth here, in the Altai region centuries ago, my dear." Siria said. "I can give you the recipe I use, but most of the ingredients are found only here, in the Altai Mountains." She put her cup on a small table. "Tell me of your Mission. I am most interested in your service to our world."

Greg glanced at Niki, seeking reassurance that speaking of it in front of Sergi was okay. Niki nodded, and he related the purpose of the Mission and the story of its medieval beginnings. He also mentioned their concerns about The Cause taking steps toward its termination. Siria listened intently, interrupting only once when she asked more detail about the adepts who hid the Stones.

Greg nodded toward Emily. "Actually, Emily can give you more detail than me. She and Karl started this venture almost three years ago."

Siria arose, collected the empty cups and took them to the kitchen.

"What have you done about the threat of this group you call The Cause?" Siria asked.

Greg wasn't sure how to answer her. "We have only tangled with them once on this Mission, but we had a lot of confrontation in the past. Both of us are black belt Kung Fu Martial Artists, so we are able to defend ourselves. We can hopefully discourage more attempts at stopping us."

Siria gave him a stern look. "Hoping will not help you." She returned to her seat, and studied the group. "Have you a plan? What will you do to find and Activate this Stone?"

Greg squirmed a little, glanced at the others, and then met Siria's gaze. "Beyond enlisting your help, we have none."

They retired for the evening and Greg fell asleep easily. The next morning, Greg nudged Emily. "Did you hear noise outside last night?"

"Ah, no. Why?" She gave him a puzzled look.

Greg shook his head. "I don't know. I thought I heard some sounds like something treading through the snow and then falling over an object. Admittedly it was faint, but . . . there nonetheless. I even got up and opened the window. When I flashed my light over the area, I saw nothing."

"Maybe you were dreaming." She smiled. "I sure hope so."

The sun had not yet crested the mountaintop, when Sergi, Emily, and Greg finished loading the Jeep. Niki and Siria attended to last-minute details preparing the cabin for the group's absence. Almost a foot of snow covered the road, but Sergi's vehicle had seen worse. They had enough supplies for three days and all the equipment they would need. Greg looked like a purple snowman, since that was the only color of ski outfit he could find in his size. And his blue shoes set such a contrast that he was not likely to wear it in a public place. But it kept him warm and that mattered most.

The little house grew smaller as they traveled down the mountain road. Soon, the group of adventurers turned off the main road and drove through a valley for the next two hours.

"I wish I had brought my camera and tripod," said Greg, "the scenery is breathtaking, it reminds me of Switzerland." The snow covered peaks reflected the sun's rays and added a crown of beauty to the brown and tan mountains.

Emily smiled. "When I asked about that, before we left you said it would be too awkward climbing snow-covered mountains, remember?" Greg nodded.

Sergi came to a crossroad and took a route going up the side of a mountain. While they ascended, the views opened to extended vistas, and the blue sky and the golden orb within it provided excellent backdrops.

"We are here," Sergi said, as he pulled into a clearing and stopped. Except for the road and some open places, tall pine trees surrounded them. The almost flat ground gave them a great place to set up a temporary camp.

Greg used his binoculars and carefully viewed the snow and woods behind them. He wanted to continue to be aware of the possibility of The Cause following them. He then scrutinized the area they had collectively picked for their starting point with Siria's help. Using a map, Sergi's knowledge of the region, and Siria's understanding of Niki's vision, they had pieced together this starting point. Sergi had identified several peaks that he considered a match for Niki's vision of a peak with two points, and they would head to a place to view them after they set up camp and had lunch. Halfway through their meal Sergi made a suggestion.

Sergi swept the area with his long arm, pointing with a proportionally long forefinger. "There is a path near here that goes along a ridge. It would give you many chances to explore on the way to an outcrop at its end. You may see the peaks I suggested from there."

They all agreed that it sounded like a worthwhile plan. After finishing their meal, they assembled the gear they needed for their journey. Each one of them had a daypack filled with picks, small shovels, hammers, and other Stone exploring tools. They also each had tents and other gear, food, and water to stay in the mountains overnight, should they get lost or have other events occur like an unexpected snowfall. Sergi led the way on their trek along the ridge.

"Oh my god, is that an Edelweiss?" Emily moved off the path and bent down to look at the plant. "I've never seen one of these physically."

Niki smiled. "Oh yes, they are abundant in these mountains."

The path led in and out of forested areas. Sometimes they could see nothing but pine and birch trees, and other times spectacular vistas – rolling mountain ranges and high peaks, covered with crystalline snow.

Emily marveled at the ever-changing character of the mountains. "Oh, what beauty. Some of these mountains seem like ancient mounds, crowning the sky. And over there, they look like young peaks searching for identity."

They all smiled at her remark. Siria said, "I have too been both mystified and humbled by these mountains, young Emily. As you move through them and feel their energy, you will understand what I mean."

At each viewpoint they looked for an indication of a place that might qualify as a "Stone-searching" area. A mountain peak, or peaks, resembling what Niki viewed in her vision, would give them their "next step" to finding this starting point. They finally reached the end of the path that overlooked a valley, affording a wide view of 300 degrees or more. White, green, and some brown areas could be seen at different heights.

They dropped their packs, and used binoculars to scan the horizon for the mystical peaks seen in Niki's vision. Each section where apparent twin peaks appeared, Greg briefly stopped and examined the terrain nearby. He looked for flat areas so that they could traverse easily, but found snow-covered land that either smoothly melted into the next, or abruptly dropped away falling out of sight.

After a thorough search of the surrounding mountains, they agreed on two near-level plateaus relatively close together that looked promising. Each plateau was a climb from the valley below, but near peaks similar to the ones in Niki's vision. They both appeared to have twin peaks or points, and were snow covered. If they found nothing at one, they had only a mile or so to the other.

Getting to either of them, though, would not be easy. No visible path or clearing that led in either direction appeared, and both were on the opposite mountain from which they stood. This meant they would have to go down into the valley between the mountains to get to the one displaying the peaks they looked for.

Sergi remembered a trail leading into the valley about halfway back to the Jeep. "It may not even be accessible anymore, but we can look for it. Once we get down to the foot of those mountains, we can find ways to access one, or both, of the plateaus you want to investigate."

They gathered their gear and followed Sergi back down the trail.

Thirty minutes later, after searching several areas that looked like their path, Sergi said, "Here is the path we are seeking." He turned away from the trail, and then brushed away snow and leaves from some pine trees.

They followed him as he made his way down a slope. At the bottom of the hill they stopped and took a break, while Sergi examined the mountain they would have to climb.

"I see no visible trails to that flat area up there that we seek, so we will have to create our own. This is not so difficult; we make a zigzag straight up the side of the mountain." He pointed toward the steep slope. "It will be a bit hard at first, but it will be much shorter than looking for another way."

They put on their snowshoes. Greg would rather have taken an easier path, but knew they had to get back to the camp before dark; so speed became more important. After almost two hours of climbing they reached the flat part of the mountain Greg had seen through his binoculars. He estimated that they were halfway up the mountain and could see the peaks spotted earlier. The larger part of the mountain below the peaks could house caves that could lead to the mysterious waterfalls in Niki's vision. As they traversed the flat area the peaks grew closer, but they saw no caves; at least not from where they stood. They took a well-deserved break, removed their snowshoes, and discussed their next steps.

Niki discovered tracks of a large wolf that looked relatively fresh. Siria bent down to touch the track, her long, white hair brushing her shoulder and almost touching the snow. She moved her fingers within the paw print, and then stopped. With fingers still on the print, she closed her eyes.

"It is Niki's white wolf," she said matter-of-factly.

"You mean from her journey?" Emily asked.

Siria traced the side of a print with her finger. "Many times visions and experiences within a journey will foretell a future encounter. I was not sure this would be so, until now."

"So you think it is worthwhile to follow these tracks?" Emily asked.

Siria peered out across the white field. "Yes. They are our path to the cave."

They followed the tracks across the flat and sloping parts of the mountain. During their trek, as the terrain changed, it led them into a horseshoe-shaped, canyon. Greg felt as if the sides of the mountain's walls closed around him like King Kong hugging him. The tracks followed a path leading upward, and when they rounded a corner, two black arches of natural stone set against the mountain, rose from the snow.

Emily gasped, "My God, they're beautiful."

"They look like entrances to cathedrals I saw years ago in Europe," Greg said.

"Look, the paw prints lead toward the arched hole on the left," Niki said.

Excited, they nearly ran to the entrance that towered 30 or 40 feet above them. Emily peered into the blackness. Boulders lay everywhere, like some giant had thrown them at the cave entrance trying to close it. They climbed over the rocks, some snow-covered, others coated with ice, following the tracks on the smaller stones, until they were about 100 feet inside. The tracks ended abruptly where the snow gave way to the cave's drier interior.

They used their lights, illuminating the cave's interior. Some of it looked like solid rock, forming a tunnel, while other parts resembled the same loose boulders spilling out onto the mountain slope. The cave's temperature felt colder due to their being out of the sun, but would probably change the further they got into the cave.

As they began the "Stone search" Greg said, "Niki will lead and Siria will stay close to her. The two who have seen the vision, lead."

"I will stay here, while you search," Sergi said. "That way if help is needed, I will be close by, but not a part of what happens. Also, I can guard the entrance and warn you if your pursuers arrive."

Greg scratched his cheek. "Good idea."

Niki moved through the tunnel observing every detail of the cave's walls with prompting from Emily, and a few words of encouragement from Greg. Since Niki was the Recipient, she would be more "in tune" with the Stone than the rest. The Stone could be hidden anywhere, and thus they all had to move with a heightened awareness. Siria kept quiet, but ever vigilant, searching every foot of the cave with all of her senses. Emily and Greg weren't sure what to look for, but gave Niki guidance when she asked.

Even after an hour into the journey, moisture still clung to the rock walls. The mountains got a lot of precipitation, but Greg didn't think it would affect the cave this far inside.

They stopped to rest. But before Greg sat on his chosen boulder, he saw paw prints on the stone floor ahead of him. "Siria, what are these?"

"They are the White Wolf's prints," Siria said. "The one that guides us." She looked up. "I sense water falling just ahead."

In a moment of quiet Greg could hear the faint sound of water moving across rocks. Was it his imagination, ignited by the power of suggestion from Siria's comments? It *could* account for so much moisture in the cave.

They continued their trek, and within minutes they all heard the sound of trickling water. About twenty minutes later, they found water running down a huge black boulder. It formed a pool, and then ran off into a crevice. Greg saw the reflection of a white wolf in the pool, its haunting blue eyes staring back at him. He raised his head to find the source of the reflection, but found only a rock wall.

When he turned back to the pool, the wolf's reflection was gone. He gave Siria a wide-eyed stare, and a chill ran down his spine.

"You thought the wolf physical?" she said, noting his puzzled look. "It can be, but like us, it is multi-dimensional. We see it in physical form when we need to, but it leads us symbolically, spiritually to our goal." She turned to the others. "We are at the place of the hidden Stone we seek. Niki, it is your time."

The black rock lay at the end of the tunnel they had followed. They removed their gear, while Niki and Siria sat across from each other, eyes closed; apparently, sensing Niki's Stone's energy; Niki felt connected with the Stone and its uniqueness, while Siria lent her innate ability to sense energy fields. Emily and Greg waited, trying to sense an energy difference until they saw the two standing near the pool.

"We have seen the Stone," Niki said. She turned and faced the black boulder. "It is behind the water."

"Behind the water? You mean in or behind that huge rock?" Greg said, pointing at what looked like part of the mountain, and certainly not moveable by them.

"Yes, maybe behind the rock, or within it, or around it. The vision did not give us a precise location, but it is definitely behind water." Niki slid her hand over the smooth, wet surface of the boulder. The water flowed from an invisible source at the crevice between the wall and roof of the cave. It then spread down the wall where it contacted the boulder, trickling into the clear, teardrop shaped pool below.

Emily examined one side of the rock while Greg checked the other. Maybe there was some way of getting inside of it, or at least a piece of it.

"The water comes from up there," Niki pointed to a place near the ceiling. "Maybe we need to discover the source."

Emily surveyed the top and bottom of the black rock. "Greg, why don't I sit or kneel on your shoulders and dig around up there?"

Sounded good to him, so up she went. Now she could almost touch the ceiling, and had access to a large area near it. She pulled a small chisel and hammer from her fanny pack, and broke into the rock formation.

While Emily chipped into the rock, she put a plastic protector over her eyes to avoid flakes of rock, Greg turned his head as much as he could to avoid splinters dropping into his eyes. She explored the whole area with her chisel, finding nothing. Emily called to Greg. "I need to get higher. Hold me while I get on my knees." Greg found it more awkward to hold her, but it enabled Emily to reach the ceiling and a crevice where the water emerged.

After a few minutes, Emily asked to get down. "The crevice looks much wider behind where the water comes out and flows down the rock face. I think there's something behind this rock, or wall, like another tunnel or room." Emily circled the rock. "It looks like a boulder from the front, but when I view it from different angles, it's actually a rounded piece of the wall sticking out from the rest."

Siria agreed that there was an opening behind the wall. "I envisioned a hollow place, like a broom closet, behind this rock."

They launched an intensive search for a way of getting behind the wall, or moving something out from it. During their search, Emily found some markings along one part of the wall joining the boulder.

"This looks like a window or part of this wall with something running through the center." Emily ran her finger over the 'diagram'. "Our ancestors hid this Stone well."

Then, behind her, Siria pointed to a place near the marks. "Look here."

They found what looked like a vein of gold running through the wall, top to bottom. "This must be what the line through the center of this drawing is telling us." Emily followed the view to the top of the wall.

Greg chipped at it, and flakes fell away from the whole vein, revealing a crack. They used their hammers to force the chisels deep into the crack. Then they pried open a hunk of wall that moved, revealing a slim opening. The energy in the cave changed like a swarm of bees flying out of the crack.

Siria and Niki hugged, and then Niki peeked into the crack. "Oh my. There it is - your closet, Siria. I feel energized, lifted, as soon as the wall opened. It must be the Stone's energy."

"Yes!" Emily said. "Feel the energy."

Greg wiped sweat from his face. "Wow. What a relief to discover the Stone's location so easily."

Fortunately Niki was slim, and slipped into the opening easily. They handed her a light and chipping tool after she squeezed behind the boulder.

"It is much dryer here," Niki said, while she brushed away earth covering the rock surface in front of her. "I feel strong energy in my chest. It seems to be coming from an overhang sticking out from the rest of the wall. Yes, I feel it moving up to my neck when I get closer to it. Give me a hammer." They did. After a couple of clanks from the hammer, Niki said, "It is loose."

They fell silent for a few moments while she worked with the overhang trying to pry it from the wall. Then a loud crash resounded from the crevice when the rock fell to the floor.

Following the noise, Niki responded with, "Oh" just above a whisper. "There...there is a light inside. Wait, it is coming from a pouch. Oh!"

Greg felt the energy increase. After a minute of quiet, a couple more "oh's" echoed from within the crevice. Then she emerged from the hole, her eyes sparkling, and held a leather pouch just above her breasts. The energy seemed even more intense and a gold light tinged with silver, encircled her upper body and head.

"I feel like a princess who has found her prince," Niki said, holding the pouch against her heart. She sat beside the pool, holding the pouch in her lap, and carefully unlaced the twine at its top and opened the pouch. The light coming from the pouch increased around her at first, and then spread over the cave. They dowsed their lanterns and beheld the brilliant multi-colored, rainbow hues emanating from the pouch. Niki then held out her palm and emptied the contents of the pouch into it.

When the Stone struck her hand, she almost dropped it. Greg realized that tremendous energy flowed into Niki from the Stone. He could feel it standing ten feet from her. Even Siria looked dazzled by the golden-silver Stone.

Emily closed her eyes and put her palms towards Niki. The Stone seemed to consume her whole body. It was as if she were part of Niki's experience.

Niki put the Stone back in the pouch, and then tied the pouch to a necklace. She put the assembly inside her shirt and buttoned it at her neck. They put their parkas back on, gathered their gear, and hiked toward the entrance. This time, Greg led the way and Emily followed at the rear.

An hour later they found themselves back outside with Sergi. It had begun to snow and he was anxious to get back to his vechicle. The new snow made the downhill trek even more dangerous, and they decided to tie a rope between them. Sergi led and Niki played caboose. They wanted the most experienced "snow people" where it counted. Greg, the non-snow person, slipped twice, and had to be rescued by his comrades. Greg knew that if he wasn't careful, he could wind up with an injury that would most assuredly slow their return to Sergi's Jeep.

By the time they reached the ravine, Greg's feet and legs felt like ice. Snow had crept into the crevices of his boots, and he couldn't remove it all; especially with a near-frozen bare hand, having to remove his gloves to get to the ice. He pushed his hand back into the purple mitten knowing he'd have to deal with the ice later.

The climb back to the ridge proved almost as difficult as their trek from the plateau. Two inches of fresh snow lay on the older crust, and it deepened by the minute. The wind blew harder, splashing large flakes into their faces. Since their original tracks were covered, and the path ended before their 'camp' area; a wrong turn could lead them into oblivion.

Darkness crept in and Sergi upped the pace. He, too felt the urgency of getting to the 'camp' before dark. They stopped. Sergi scrutinized the area in front of him, trying to find some sign guiding them to the path they needed. Tension gripped his face and voice.

"We are close, but there is no clear path to follow. The ridge ends here, and now there is just flat land. If we make a wrong turn we could be out here for days. And in this weather, maybe not get back at all."

The troubled look on Niki's and Emily's faces mirrored Greg's growing concern about not making the last Activation in time. Or worst, not getting back at all.

Siria came forward. "Maybe I can be of assistance. I sense the path of energy we left when we came this way. If it has not disbursed too much, we can follow it back to the camp. We go that way," she said, pointing a little to the left of their current path.

"Good," Sergi said, and moved in that direction.

"Isn't it great not only having an experienced mountain escort, but also a shaman for a guide?" Greg said, falling in behind Sergi. Niki and Emily nodded, smiling a little. Still, Greg felt a sense of foreboding, of danger lurking in the whitened forest, which now was turning gray. What little daylight they had left, before darkness crept into their pathway, slowly faded.

Sergi lit his light, and Greg his, while Siria led the way. She stopped often, trying to sense the energy and its trail to their campsite. Twice, she stopped and meditated after losing her awareness of which way to turn. Greg felt lost and distressed about their plight and sensed the same disappointment among the others.

Finally, Siria stopped and motioned for them to stand around her. "I have lost the trail. The energy has faded too much for me to sense its former path. I suggest we make a camp here until daylight. We can find dry kindling under the snow where larger brush keeps it dry."

They dumped their gear, and prepared spaces for a fire and their tents. Siria found dry kindling and Niki gathered dry logs for a fire. It amazed Greg that the stuff was still dry and they knew where to find it. While searching for the "dry kindling," Greg thought about their situation and the clock ticking away. His hands trembled as he carried the wood – not just from icy cold eating through his gloves, but his sense of not making the 'target' date of 11-11-2011, given to them through the Stone's Book 2; failing the most important task he'd ever been given.

Once they got the fire going, they erected their tents, and prepared their evening meal. Anything hot would be welcome tonight. The snow eased somewhat and made tending to the fire easier. They sat as close to the fire as they dared, soaking in its heat. Greg was so glad that they had packed tents in their equipment after objecting to carrying so much through the heavy snow.

The women were discussing what they might expect when they looked for an activation site for Niki's Stone.

"We will do similar activities as we did today," said Emily. "But the Activation Ceremony will be much more intensive."

After a few quiet moments, Greg said. "If we ever get out of here."

16

MT SHASTA

arl's flight to Sacramento felt restful, and gave him a chance to go over the details of the course manual he had prepared for Jasmine. Since he had little training as a teacher, he felt bringing Jasmine into the teacher's circle would benefit the company. Emily had trained Jasmine a week before Greg left for Calcutta, but did not get a chance to officially help Jasmine launch her first class. So Karl took on the responsibility to make that happen.

After climbing into his rental car, Karl began his drive to Mt. Shasta up a winding road that kept him alert and aware of the passing scenery. Glimpsing at the high desert plains below gave him a view of a different terrain than he had seen in the mountains along California's coast. As the mountain city sat over three thousand feet above Sacramento, the car climbed throughout the drive. When Karl arrived at the restaurant where he was to meet Jasmine, he got out and stretched. He felt both tired and a bit stressed from maneuvering some hairpin curves on his way up the mountain road.

"Hi, you must be Karl," a petite Jasmine said while opening the restaurant door.

Karl smiled and reached out his hand. "Yep it's me. Here to help you start your new career, so to speak. Glad to finally meet you."

"I am so happy to be getting a chance to actually teach all that I learned during the past couple of years." She led Karl into the café.

They chatted during their meal, and Karl asked her about what she had learned from her adventure here two years ago searching for the pink Stone.

"Oh, it moved from mysterious, to frightening, to joyful and back again." Jasmine said. "Visiting Telos had to be the most mysterious trip of my life. Whoa, what a ride." She went on to explain her abduction and almost losing the Stone.

Later she led Karl to the new classroom. It was part of a small hotel, giving the students both lodging and other facilities they would need during the classes. "I suggest you take a room here to facilitate your getting to the classes during the week. They have three floors, so you have plenty to choose from."

"Sounds good to me." Karl scanned the classroom. "Looks like it will serve our purpose. Shall we get started on the manual?"

They spent the next two hours going over the new teacher manual, so that Jasmine would feel comfortable with it in the morning.

"This is the first class manual, but has it been updated?" Jasmine asked.

Karl pointed to the manual. "Yes, we have used it for the past couple of years and seemed like it needed polishing as we continue to learn more about our spiritual selves."

Afterwards, Jasmine left and Karl checked into the hotel, ready to monitor the morning class.

The next morning, Karl breathed in the crisp mountain air, while he took a walk up the street and back to the café. After a sumptuous breakfast, he met with Jasmine before the students arrived to assure she was prepared. He then sat in the back as the students showed up. The classroom was smaller than the one in Sedona with only twelve chairs. But Jasmine's teaching style kept her moving around the room stopping at the whiteboard and desk to attend to instructions and demonstrations.

"Good morning. My name is Jasmine and I will be your teacher for the next few days. You are about to embark on a journey with no distance; a journey in your mind. You might say that you have entered a new level of learning, because the ideas you will grow to understand this week are not taught elsewhere."

Jasmine opened the manual and asked everyone to introduce themselves. Afterward they all turned to the first pages. "We have been taught all our lives to depend on someone else to lead the way. Most of us believe we are great followers, but not leaders. You have within you the same qualities and powers that anyone else has; you have the same potentials and abilities. You most likely would not be here today if you really believed what I am saying. Why? Because you would be out there doing what you wanted to do, no questions asked. You are here today, because you both believe that there is something more, but also that you are not good enough."

She moved to the middle of the room and used her hands as she spoke. "Now most of you would probably deny the last part of that statement and think you are capable of anything; but your sub-conscious mind knows otherwise. And this is what we are here to work on this week – your unconscious mind. If you think that you are consciously running your life, you might be surprised as we get into the material today. Your conscious mind might be compared to your car, the vehicle, but your subconscious mind is like *you* driving the car. In other words, just as you are the driver of the car, your unconscious mind is the driver and controls what you think and do."

Karl listened intently, picking up on the direction Jasmine was headed. He liked the way she moved through the material in such a sure and confident way. He could tell by the students' body language that many of them felt uncomfortable with the ideas Jasmine presented.

Jasmine went on to explain how we learn from other people and grasp ideas and beliefs from the people who are around us as we move through life, especially as a child. "What we must do when we reach a certain point is unlearn what we have been taught, so to speak, and teach ourselves a new and better way to live. Not a simple task, she emphasized as she answered questions. They then took a break.

As the students returned, Jasmine stood at a table in the front of the classroom. "For the rest of today, we will discuss personal responsibility. This is a subject with many facets relating to your everyday lives. The first thing about personal responsibility is that we create our lives in every moment, albeit from our unconscious minds. No one else can create your life for you, although there may be teachers and guides along the way who help you make wise choices."

A hand went up. "If we are totally responsible for what happens in our lives, doesn't that make us alone with no help from others?"

Jasmine moved to the front row of chairs. "Well, I guess you could look at it that way, but it is a bit more complex than that. First, you are never alone, since you are surrounded by Angels, guides, and the Universe or God, at all times. Second, you can get help from other people at any time, but you are responsible for whatever you are doing. If someone helps you and makes a mistake, you are still responsible for the outcome, and need to take care of it in whatever way you are led. Don't forget you are moving through life dealing with what others have taught you. Does that answer your question?"

The student nodded. "I guess I will learn more about this new way of seeing things as the week goes on."

"It may take longer than this week." Jasmine winked at him. "I am only here to give you the fundamentals. It is up to you to work with what you learn in order to live from this foundation."

The rest of the day, Jasmine taught more on personal responsibility, especially how we are the sole creators of our lives, and the ways in which we go about this creation. She ended the class with homework to practice what they had learned, and preparation for the next day's class on "Acceptance".

17

ALTAI MOUNTAINS

reg unzipped the top of the tent and peeked through the opening at the white canopy of sky above him. A gray dawn eased its way across the mountains, spilling clouds onto the snow-filled treetops. He crawled out onto the frozen ground. Light snow fell like feathers from a torn pillow, snuffing the fire's last embers. Sergi had already taken down his tent and was putting it into its bag. Sergi glanced his way and smiled.

"Good morning, my friend," Sergi said. "We have some work to do, yes?"

Greg nodded. He knew "work" meant finding Sergi's Jeep and getting back to Siria's cabin before they froze in this white wasteland. The others joined them, while Greg lit his pack stove to heat water for warm drinks.

"I heard from my Stone last night," Niki said. "It confirmed for me that my shamanic journey was indeed a preview of finding and activating my Stone. So we will need to find another waterfall and the cave behind it for my Activation ceremony."

"For that," Siria said. "You have the good fortune of help from our second white wolf, and maybe the leopard."

Greg frowned. "Right. We only have to determine the area, and get to it. But, right now, it's the 'get to it' part that bothers me." They finished their hot drinks and snacks and searched for their next steps.

Remembering that the sun was behind them when they left camp and the Jeep, they decided to head toward the sun. It was about the same time of day, perhaps an hour earlier than when they began their trek to find the Stone. Of course, it was possible they had already passed the Jeep area, but nothing else made sense at the moment. The flurries increased to a wet, stinging snow that bit into Greg's face, obliterating the glowing sphere they followed. Their ability to see more than twenty feet ahead made Greg feel that they might have just as well continued the night before.

"Let us join hands." Sergi said. "It will help us stay together and give us a solid line for our search."

They clasped hands as Sergi suggested, while they searched for the Jeep. Greg was at the far end of the line, not because he wanted to be there, but because he was the last one to join hands. Just as Greg was about to suggest they stop, his knee hit something hard and pain sent him to the ground with a moan. The others stopped, and Niki, who was closest to Greg, bent down to help.

"Really hurts," Greg said. "It felt like I hit metal." He reached over to where he'd run into the object. "A bumper. I ran into a bumper," he shouted.

Niki put her hands on the hood of Sergi's Jeep and shouted, "We have found it. We've found it." and laughed. Jumping and yelling, they all gathered around Greg and the snow laden vehicle and began digging it out of the snow. An hour later, the snow slowed, so that Sergi could see well enough to drive, and they headed back toward Siria's cabin. Sergi needed four-wheel drive all the way back on the new, unpacked snow.

When they got within a half mile of the cabin, Siria said, "We need to stop. I sense intruders ahead."

"Intruders, like people or animals?" Niki asked.

Siria rubbed her hands together. "I believe it to be human." She turned towards Greg and Emily. "The group you call The Cause you spoke of may have arrived. We need to be cautious."

"I really was not expecting someone this far away from 'civilization' so to speak." Emily said. "But I guess I am not surprised either."

Greg turned toward Niki. "We need to make some adjustments."

They proceeded cautiously toward the cabin. As they pulled up along side of the structure, they decided to act as if they suspected nothing. But Emily and Greg had already fine tuned their Kung Fu moves, and the rest had grabbed large tree braches dug out of the snow. Using them as hiking sticks, the crew entered the cabin.

"Greetings comrades, put your hands in the air." There were three men, one in front and two on either side, holding revolvers. "I am Gavin, the man you will need to deal with today. We have been waiting for you all night. You must have had a long journey." He strolled around the group eyeing each person. "I know you two, you are too old, so the Stone person must be one of you two." He pushed Niki and Sergi toward his partners who pointed guns at the group. "Search them."

While Gavin kept his gun on the group, the other two searched Niki first. While she squirmed and resisted every move, they removed her heavy jacket, then her leather shirt, and finally her blouse. "Here is want we want," said the man and grabbed the pouch hanging from Niki's neck.

"No. It is a precious gem of my grandmother." She grabbed the pouch with both hands. "No, please." The other man pulled her arms in back of her, while his comrade pulled the leather strap over her head. They pushed Niki away and handed the pouch to Gavin.

He opened the pouch and emptied the stone into his hand. "So this is what you people worked so hard to find. My comrades never saw the one you found at Stonehenge. But now we know what they look like." He lifted his arm so the other two could see the stone more closely. "So pretty." He laughed. "It is too bad we have to dispose of it." His mouth curled up into cruel smirk.

Gavin grabbed a hammer and put the stone on the brick fireplace. Greg and Emily dove at the distracted men disarming the two, but too late to stop Gavin as he smashed the stone to bits. Niki screamed and whole room came alive with seven people diving for the three guns and trying to take control.

When the dust cleared, the three intruders were tied individually and together. The authorities were called. In the meantime Niki kept trying to put the pieces of the stone back together, moaning during the process. She had to put on a big show for the three intruders, because she could not reveal to them that the *real* Stone was safely hidden. If they knew they failed, The Cause would continue their pursuit. If the gold-silver Stone had been destroyed, Mission 2 would fail and that would be the end of their quest.

The authorities arrived an hour later, and took the three away on counts of breaking and entering, theft, and attempted manslaughter.

Siria finally prepared the hot meal they had wanted when they arrived. Over a late lunch they discussed an area south of Siria's cabin. Meanwhile, Greg pulled Niki's real Stone from a hidden compartment in his shoe, covered with a clay and pebble concoction to disperse its energy, and gave it to her.

"Oh thank you for such a great idea." Niki beamed. "The stone I used was indeed my grandmother's, but I am sure she is glad it was sacrificed for a 'greater cause'." They all smiled, while she moved to the sink and cleaned the Stone.

"We will have to do something about them knowing where we are going. But right now we have a Stone to Activate," Greg said.

"I have seen a vision of your Activation site." Siria looked up from her soup at Niki. "It is further south of your Stone's hiding place and at the twin peaks you saw in your vision."

Niki held the Wisdom Stone in cupped hands and closed her eyes. After a few moments, she looked up. "Yes, my Stone agrees with the location Siria. Wow, we have double confirmation of the Activation site."

"That is the way the Stones work." Emily glanced at Niki. "The Stone guides you from the time you first hold it until it is Activated. You can depend on that."

Sergi put his bowl in the sink. "I am not sure how far south into the area I can drive. I drove through it a few months ago on the way to Mongolia. It did not have much snow, but even then it was not easy to maneuver my Jeep."

It appeared that they were up against a formidable opponent — the weather. But they had a formidable ally in Spirit, and the Universe. They dried out their gear, and prepared for whatever confronted them on the morrow.

As the sun rose, peaking out from an eastern mountain side, Greg watched from the Jeep's back window with mixed feelings as the bungalow disappeared. He wanted to join the exploration to find the Activation site and take part in the ceremony, but loathed the wet and cold. The weather had cleared though, and the sun and a blue sky greeted them, while they drove along the road. Niki confirmed Siria's choice through a vision while using the Stone. They drove east for awhile, and then turned south along an old logging road.

Sergi said, "Logging vehicles and equipment used this road years ago, but it has not been used for decades. Hopefully, this old gal," he patted the vehicle's door, "will get us there safely."

Jagged peaks pierced the sky all around them, while they traveled within the lap of the vast mountain region. The road wound around one mountain, and then another. They'd briefly cross a valley, then climb again around another mountain. They finally reached the area that Siria and Niki suggested they use as their base for exploration due to the flat terrain and close access to the envisioned peaks.

"Ah, we made it all the way here in my trusty Jeep." Sergi said with a smile. He patted his vehicle when they got out, thanking it for such good service.

Emily gazed at the enormity and splendor surrounding her. "It is so beautiful here. It reminds me of the magnificent Swiss Alps I visited years ago."

They set up a base camp near the Jeep, so that if they somehow returned in the dark, they would have everything ready. They packed equipment and food to stay overnight at the cave, knowing the Activation would take place at sunset.

While they ate a quick snack, Greg noted it was only 9:00. Their early start gave the group all day to find the cave. Thirty minutes later, they set off into the mountains to find the cave. Sergi didn't know the area they were about to visit, so they would have to rely on their own and Siria's intuitive sense of where to go.

Siria and Niki led the way with Sergi bringing up the rear. Greg sensed that Sergi too, felt a bit uneasy about the intuitive aspect of their journey. With several feet of snow beneath them, no visible trail led anywhere. But their guides didn't need a trail. The path to the cave was in their minds, and they needed only to follow.

They climbed slowly upward, and Greg felt grateful, remembering the steep slope of two days before and his cold feet. The sun helped with its warmth and brightness, painting the forest emerald green beneath a bonnet of snow.

The gradual part of the climb lasted for an hour, and then they switched direction. Siria led them across a ridge that connected two mountains. Once on the other side, their ascent grew steeper, although not as much so as the one a couple of days before. They finally came upon a plateau, where they stopped and had another snack. They had decided to have small meals while travelling rather than larger ones that took extra time to prepare, and clear afterward. They welcomed the hot tea and its easy preparation over their small propane burner. An ocean of snow around them provided all the water they needed.

While Greg drank his tea, a sense of déjà vu crept into his mind. A few yards away he spotted animal tracks, just as he had seen before finding the first cave. Niki arrived at them just as he rose from his snow-laden rock to investigate. She stooped and examined them with great care.

"It is our white wolf," she said with a smile.

Emily said, "Yes!" And the others stood and clapped.

Greg followed the tracks with his eyes for as far as he could, and saw them disappear behind a massive outcrop of boulders and jagged rock. They finished their drinks, put on their packs, and followed the tracks. When they rounded the huge rock-pile the plateau narrowed into a ridge and sloped downward. They followed the trail for another 30 minutes or so, when the pathway widened and leveled again, and they saw the enormous mouth of a cave. Greg stared at the opening, amazed at its size. He figured it to be at least 50 feet high and 30 feet wide.

When they entered the huge opening, it reminded Emily of creepy movies she had seen as a kid. There were no bats flying around, but the cave did have stalactites and ledges everywhere. They strolled through the cavern exploring its crevices with their lights. It did not become smaller like the other caves Greg had recently seen, but remained large like the ones he'd experienced in the States as a kid.

Wet paw prints led the way as before. The deeper they got into the cavern, the more amazing it appeared. The ledges' size and number increased, as did the stalactites. Vast curvatures of rock emerged both concave and convex in form, carving out huge sculptures above them. Ridges and crevices ran along the floor, and weaved through the cave while the group picked their way among them. They came to one such crevice directly in their path and ten or twelve feet across. The route continued on the other side, but they saw no way to go except directly across the huge hole. On either side the walls climbed right to the ceiling.

"We need something to cross on," Greg said, searching the cave, "like a long board."

Emily took a rope from her pack. "A rope would work. But we need something we can reach to tie it on."

"I can jump across," Niki said, studying the crevice.

Greg first studied her then the crevice. "Assuming you can, how do the rest of us join you?"

"Like Emily said, we can use rope. I can tie it to a rock or stalagmite, and you can swing across." She must have picked up his look, for she continued. "No, really you *can*, it's easy."

"Niki, this is not a broad-jump pit," Sergi said, his hands on his hips. "The floor is wet on both sides and nothing but rock. You also have on bulky clothes and shoes; do you really think you can get across safely?"

"Yes. It is not that far. I have jumped much farther — under better conditions of course, but it still is not a big deal for me. I'll take off my snowsuit; it will be easy. Just give me some room and plenty of light on both sides." She backed away from the edge a few feet, testing the slipperiness of the floor. She removed her jacket and then her heavy pants, and moved into position to jump. They all lit their lights, shinning two on one side and two on the other.

"Ready," she said, in a stooped position. Then she took three long, running steps and leaped. Greg held his breath while her body sailed through the darkness, waiting for her boots to touch the other side. Then he heard a 'clunk' followed by "oof." Niki had landed on the other side with room to spare, and they all cheered and applauded her feat.

"Thank you," she said, breathing heavily, and standing, facing them. "Throw me one end of a rope."

Sergi knotted one end of his and threw it to her. "Now tie your end to my pack, put my clothes inside and swing it over to me." She then got her lantern out of the pack and used its glow to find a place to tie the rope. After a few minutes, she crawled up on a ledge about ten or twelve feet above the floor, and tied the rope around a huge rock, which she tested for its strength.

"Let's start with Siria. She is the lightest, and her swing across will give me an indication of the sturdiness of this rock," she said, pulling on the rope before she threw the end to them.

Siria swung without a problem, her feet landing squarely on the rocky floor a couple of feet or so beyond the edge. Emily swung next.

"Okay, Greg, your turn," Niki said, and a chill went through him.

While swinging across did not bother him, it was landing on the cold, slippery floor that did. He felt the cold, dampness from the floor creep up his legs while he ran, and gripped the rope. He landed on the other side easily.

Sergi sent the rest of the packs over the hole, and then swung himself over. They sat for a few moments, drinking water and recovering from their ordeal. With everything intact, they shouldered their packs and trekked further into the cavern. Within minutes, the tracks disappeared, and they heard water falling into water. They rounded a corner, and beheld a breathtaking sight. Like a scene from a fairytale in some mystical land, a waterfall flowed from high in the ceiling to a large pool, and was lit by a magical golden-white light from somewhere behind it. When they got closer, they saw a white figure within the misty, falling water, and behind it a cave entrance; the source of the illumination.

The light cast a halo around the figure, and a golden aura around every drop of falling water. The figure seemed both etheric and physical the way it moved through the water and danced in the light. It put out its hand, as if pointing, and on the rocks below lay a white leopard right in front of the pool. It too, had a golden aura around it. Niki strode toward the pool of water below the falls, where sparkling drops bounced upon its surface. A rainbow arched above it, linked with the human-sized figure and leopard. Niki stood watching and waiting, when the white wolf appeared from her left, out of the falls, and sat beside her. Greg knew that her shamanic vision was complete. The Stone would go into the cave behind the falls for Activation.

Niki made her way behind the falls followed by the wolf. Emily and Greg followed, and Siria sat at the cave's entrance, cross-legged, in a trance, supporting Niki's mission in the cave. Sergi returned to the entrance to wait and set up a camp for the night's stay.

The white wolf went ahead of Niki into the cave, which seemed dark after leaving the light of the falls. But they could see the white wolf through the darkness; it seemed to glow and lit their way through a narrow passage of the cave. The three followed for about 20 minutes, before coming to a great room, similar to the cavern they had just left. A soft light illumined the room that had no visible source, like a back-lit stage. To get a detailed view, Greg and the others checked the room with their lights, but when light hit the wall they had just entered — the access-way had disappeared! It was as if they had come through a portal that now was closed to the outside.

Deeper into the 'room' they found themselves surrounded by altars that looked like white marble, similar to those Greg had seen in Greece. He counted five of them, with one in the center larger than the others, and rising higher above the floor. The other altars were round and oval shapes, but this one had alternating points and curves around it. Niki chose that one for her Golden-Silver Stone and gently set it on the altar's center. She knelt before it, honoring its beauty and sacredness. When she did, the white figure they had seen in the falls appeared, and the Stone glowed. It gave off golden-silver light that filled the area around the altar, and then spread throughout the room.

"I am Estival," the figure said. "I bring you greetings from many worlds and my own, Sirius. Your friend Siria is from my world as well and we have communicated many times." They all gazed at each other, mouths open and eyes wide. The figure smiled and sent Siria a telepathic "hello". "I have waited within this beautiful Stone for this moment long enough. It is time to cast its light upon your world. Please join me in song."

While they sang, the room filled with music, and golden-silver light danced with it. "We dance to the golden light, we dance to the silver light, and we see them flow into one." After they finished the mantra, Estival directed Niki to begin gathering five gems and place each on its appointed altar. Then the wolf reappeared. It stood to one side near the back of the room. Niki intuitively knew to go to the wolf, reached underneath its belly, and pulled from between two rocks the first gem: a blue sapphire. When she touched the stone, the wolf disappeared. She took the stone to the left-most altar, remembering the placement of gems from deep within her vision. She placed it at the center, then kissed it and bowed, backing away.

Estival spoke again. "The sapphire represents the Blue Ray of Structure of all that is holy; the spiritual essence of all that is good. It supports the other elements and connecting points on the Web-of-Life."

Niki then turned, and saw the wolf standing on the *other* side near the back, and again intuitively knew what to do. Below it she found another blue sapphire: the second gem. She took it to the right-most altar, again bowed to it and blew upon it.

Estival said. "What do you see, Niki?"

"I see a pyramid, with the two sapphires as its base and the Golden-Silver Stone as its apex," Niki said. "This vision must represent what I am creating here."

The wolf appeared again, on the left nearer the next altar. Niki again knew from her vision what to do. She approached it, and under its belly laid a ruby. She took it and the wolf vanished. She placed the glistening gem on the next altar, and ceremoniously kissed it, honoring the stone.

Estival spoke. "This ruby represents the Red Ray of Birth. It is the beginning, the Alpha of all of Life. Birth is always new, and re-Birth re-news all that would be transformed." Estival and Niki then performed a ceremony, blessing the gem and singing a mantra, joined by Greg and Emily. "We sing to the red and blue, we dance to building life and rebirth."

The wolf appeared near the last altar. Niki again knowingly approached it and reached below its belly to find an emerald. She took it to the last altar and placed it at its middle, bowed and backed away.

Estival appeared and moved behind it, then spoke again. "The emerald represents the Green Ray of Harmony. Without harmony, nothing lives, for it honors all of Life. The Universe cannot exist without harmony. The tiniest atom cannot function

without harmony. It is the glue that holds All That Is in place."
Estival performed another ceremony to bless the stone with white
light that seemed to flow from her hands. They all celebrated
with dance and song. "We dance to the green ray, we sing a song
of harmony for it is who we are."

Niki stepped back, away from the altars, and Estival settled
behind them all, while a rainbow formed over the altars. The ends
were on the sapphires, the center over the Golden-Silver Stone.
This tied all of the symbolic gems together.

Niki again spoke of her pyramid vision. "Now the two sapphires
are at its base, the ruby on the left halfway up, the emerald on the
right halfway up, and the Golden-Silver Stone at its apex. A light is
flowing out of the pyramid's capstone – golden-silver, surrounded
by a golden aura. This pyramidal structure combines the gems
used giving me strength to carry on with honor for me and others
I will touch."

Music flowed through the room — the most beautiful, harmonious, melodious music Emily had ever heard. The wolf appeared
for the last time near the main altar. Under its belly Niki found
two diamonds, and the wolf vanished. As directed, she placed a
diamond on either side of the Golden-Silver Stone. A white light
haloed by golden-silver light emerged from it, and the energy in
the room increased so much that the three participants had to
brace themselves against the walls. The whole room vibrated while
Estival raised her arms and spoke.

*"This Stone calls the Gold and Silver Ray of Honor. Feel the quality
of Honor move within this room. Feel it thread its way through your
body as it permeates the Earth. Honor lifts you high in wholeness. It
melds integrity and respect. Honor touches the depth of your Being,
releasing that melding. You reach out, and as you honor others, you
honor yourself. Honoring all of Life and treating it with respect brings
it to you when it becomes a part of you. You will then move about the
Earth with Honor, in Honor.*

*Mother Earth has honored you by allowing your presence. She has
supplied your world with resources for food, energy, and materials, and*

withstood irresponsible actions using them. She has opened herself to all of you, and given her all. Now it is time for the people of this world to honor Mother Earth. She is ailing, and needs the help of every being on her surface. Why is Honor only something you hear about in high places? Surely each of you here honors the other, yet how few in your world speak of honor and look upon another with honor?"

Estival spread her 'arms,' causing the Gold and Silver Ray to widen and encompass everyone in the room; so that each could feel the energy and be truly honored by it.

"Return to Honor. Lift it to the place where it belongs, and lift your soul as well. No one can deny your Honor. To dishonor another is to dishonor yourself. The insect honors the plant from which it feeds, while the plant honors the insect by giving it food. The sky honors the bird that flies, while the bird honors the sky with its song. God, the Source of All honors you as its Expression. How can you not honor God?

Everything is God, the Great All in All. There is nothing that is not God. How then can you not honor it all? Mother Earth is waiting. God is waiting. Your own Soul is waiting. Move to the place of Honor, and the healing will begin."

Estival then hummed harmoniously with the three dancers still singing, and the gold and silver Stone itself vibrated. The vibration increased, and felt to Emily like the tremor from an earthquake moving across the room and dislodging bits of dirt from the ceiling. Estival raised her hands toward the sky that lay beyond the rock ceiling, and the three stopped.

Silence filled the air, vibrating with everything else in the room. The vibration grew so intense that they sat on the floor to keep from falling. The intensity of the light grew as well, and it looked like a thousand suns lit the space. They put their hands out in front of their faces to soften the intense light. In the midst of the powerful vibrations and light, the three compatriots drifted into deep meditation.

Estival then turned, facing the altars and her arms became as giant wings, covering all of them like a white veil. Music, light, and energetic vibrations filled the room. The three joined the celebration, dancing and singing with unabashed joy and with reverence. Then, slowly, the level of the music and light diminished until a quiet glow filled each of the altars.

Estival once again appeared as an illumined figure, stood in front of the main altar and bowed. "I stand here to guard this most Sacred Stone; it is my task. Thank you for your service and love. Go in peace."

Again, as in England, the Stone's Being spoke to Emily and told her that their next site was Borobudur in Java. She was to contact Shali in Singapore.

The White Leopard appeared at the passageway's entrance and rendered it visible. The beast led the now-sobered humans through the entry-way. When they looked back, no evidence of an entrance remained — only rock walls. Upon reaching the falls, the leopard vanished. Beads of sweat covered Greg's forehead while he watched tears stream down the faces of Niki and Emily through his own.

"Truly, I am transformed," Niki said. "My shamanic journey has come true." When Niki stepped down from the falls, a golden aura surrounded her. She moved like a princess, and almost floated down the rocky path like an angel. She and the others found Siria and gave her warm hugs. The Shaman's mystical presence, coupled with the magical aura of the three caused a golden glow to surround them all.

"My, what a feeling." Emily smiled. "It is like being in a misty shower with golden light surrounding me."

Silently, they trekked back to Sergi at the entrance. When they arrived at the crevice, Greg felt peaceful, and knew it would be "no big deal." Sergi waited on the other side. He had latched a rope to a high and large rock on that side, and was ready for them. Greg decided to go first. He grabbed the rope with both hands, took a few steps, and hurled his body across. Sergi caught his arm when he let go of the rope, and he landed on solid ground without a hitch.

The rest made their own trips over the crevice and joyfully hiked to the camp area. It was a time for celebration, and Siria pulled out a bottle of vintage wine from her pack.

"I knew we would need this." She smiled and sunk a corkscrew into the top. Removing the cork, she then poured the wine into their drinking cups, and they performed a toast.

"To Niki, to the Golden-Silver Stone, to Honor and the Mission!" Greg laughed while five cups clunked together.

They then gave toasts for each of the participants: Sergi, Siria, Emily and Greg, for it took all of them working as a team to make the Activation successful. Again the cups came together, and they laughed and drank the refreshing wine.

After the winefest, they prepared the evening meal and talked about Honor.

"Honor is something that I have always practiced." Sergi said. "My life has always been around people who honored each other in so many ways. I guess it is standard practice with people of the mountains."

Greg wrinkled his brow. "Unfortunately, there is not much Honor practiced by those in my Country. While the government honors the military and such, honor amongst the citizens in general does not happen. I too have gotten away from honoring others due to the lifestyle I live and the consciousness around me. Our classes though are a big help in rebuilding that way of treating people."

It was a joyous occasion, like a party. Niki repeated much of her experience for Sergi, and Siria told more stories. Sergi told a few as well. Emily gazed at the four joyous beings sitting around a campfire, sipping wine, and singing songs of service to a wonderful world that needed their help.

After spending the night in the cave, they returned to Siria's cabin late in the afternoon. Emily and Greg made ready for their next trip. Unable to tell anyone exactly where they were heading, they just alluded to getting back home. Sergi took them to the train station, and they caught a train to Biisk, where they would stay overnight in preparation for their trip to Java.

That evening in the hotel room, Emily once again informed Greg of their next site by writing it down and then destroying the paper. Afterward, they discussed their next moves.

"We need to call Karl about the smashed stone." Greg said. "Then when Fitzburg listens to our conversation, he will think we have lost and maybe leave us alone."

"How do you suppose they hear our conversations?" Emily wrinkled her brow.

Greg pointed up. "There are satellites everywhere, and Fitzburg is a military commander of some sort. I am sure he has access, or knows people who have access to this kind of equipment. Then all he has to do is tune in to our telephone conversations. All he has to know is one phone number."

"Wow." Emily stared out the window. "So what do we do?"

"After we call Karl and suggest our Mission is doomed, we encrypt our conversations," Greg said. "Karl knows a guy who can fix us up with equipment. When they can no longer tap into our communications, we will be safe."

Greg dialed the satellite phone. "Hi Karl. Man have I got some news for you."

"Hi, Greg. You sound upset. What's up?"

Greg made his voice sound defeated. "You will never believe what happened. When we got back to Siria's place, the hoodlums were waiting for us with guns. They took Niki's Stone Karl, they took the Stone."

"Do they have it now?" Karl's voice sounded unsettled.

"I wish they did. No, they smashed it to smithereens. It's gone, Karl, it's gone."

Karl took a deep breath. "What do we do now?"

"We fail." Greg paused. "There may be a way around it, but I see nothing right now. We will stay here a few days and get ourselves together. Then we will head back. Sorry for the bad news, but I had to let you know. We'll talk later."

Karl acknowledged the painful situation and said he would wait. Emily caught Greg's eyes. "Now what?"

"One of us can write Karl an email, and send it tomorrow, explaining what really happened." Greg drew his eyebrows together. "We can also ask that he get the encryption phone equipment and send it to us in Java. When we get there we can rent a post office box or have it sent to the next site's address. Email might work, but the phone would give us voice confirmation that he got our messages."

Emily grabbed the laptop. "I will get busy on the email."

"Now we wait for the repercussions from The Cause and take our next steps carefully." Greg gave her a pensive look. "Meanwhile, we have another Stone to find and Activate. We need to fly to Calcutta and check in with The Council, so we can call Shali and get some cash. We don't want to use our credit cards anymore, because they can trace the hotels we stay at with them. We can fly using them, but that is all."

Emily raised her eyebrows. "Wow, this 'security' thing is more serious than I had imaged."

"If we are going to get this job done with people breathing down our necks, we have to be more careful. If they find out we are faking this smashing Stone thing, they will get really pissed, and I hate to think of the consequences."

18

SINGAPORE, MALAYSIA

The city streets seemed less busy this morning on the outskirts of east Singapore. Sun peaked through high clouds following a morning shower that usually slowed traffic in this crowded city. Shali put two arrangements of mixed flowers in the store window and watched blackbirds clear the sidewalk of rice and seed. "Big wedding yesterday. Pesky crows love it."

Her clerk, Laeli nodded. "Saves us to clean mess."

Since Shali lived in Singapore, she personally conducted her six store business from this flower shop. She made her way to the small office passing rows of multiple types of roses and lilies. *Marriage season is busy time, but these flowers take space from others. Is all good.* Shali examined the monthly spreadsheet. "Sales are up, Pungu." She ran her hand across the back of her white Persian cat, who took care of the office when her owner traveled.

Later that evening, Shali gazed out the window of her 23rd floor apartment overlooking downtown Singapore. The bright lights lit the sky, preventing any chance of star-gazing. She sometimes missed the country-like surroundings of her childhood home in Thailand.

She would lay on the grass at night with her hands folded behind her head, and gaze skyward. Shali had sometimes laid there for hours counting stars and trying to identify constellations. What a different life she led now.

"Well Pungu, another dreamy night in Singapore." She pulled the pink steel cat comb through the animal's long fur coat. "We make a great couple; you want no mate and me too. We have each other; that is enough." After the combing stopped, Pungu curled into a ball in the middle of her lap and slept. "Of course, I have no one to pamper me like you. Maybe some day."

Shali picked up the book she had laid on the end table earlier, pushed the lever on the white, faux-leather lounge chair, laid back, and relaxed. When she saw it in a book store a week before, the title intrigued her: *The Spirituality of Kung Fu*. Having earned her black belt earlier in the year, she knew about mindfulness and inner strength well enough, but this book went way beyond what she had learned. She read the brief *Introduction*.

"A martial artist uses his mind and insight first, and his physical abilities second. This premise you, as a Kung Fu practitioner, have been taught since you began. It is time to step up to a new level of understanding. There is something within you far deeper and meaningful than you know."

Shali put the book beside her and gazed at the ceiling. "I have a powerful volume here, Pungu. A must read for me every night; with you on my lap of course." She smiled at the curled up ball of fur. "But my trip to Shanghai is fast approaching, and that will take me away from you; but not the book, I promise." She lay back in the chair and closed her eyes.

The morning sun slid across the plush carpet in Shali's apartment, and then up the lounge chair until it struck her eyes. "What is that?" She sat up with a jerk and scanned the room. "Oh my, I slept in the chair all night." She turned toward the kitchen clock. "I must get ready for work, Pungu. No breakfast this morning." She readied herself for work, grabbed a quick bite and a swig of coffee, and rushed out the door with Pungu's carrier in her hand.

At lunch time, Shali jogged to the Kung Fu school she had attended every Thursday for the last four years.

"It is time for you to take your next step, Shali," said her instructor. "As a Black Belt you have both the privilege and the duty to instruct other students. This activity will earn you points toward your Black Belt degrees." She met a red belt student, whom she would work with for the next month. It gave her confidence and a great deal of pleasure to help another person attain levels of Kung Fu mastery. Knowing that she would be gone the following week, she informed her instructor and new student of her absence.

Back in her apartment that evening, Shali received an unusual phone call. "Yes, this is Shali.

The voice at the other end began both an intriguing and frightening proposal. "My name is Emily. You are needed to take part in a trip to a sacred site that I will have to explain when we meet in person." She went on to explain Mission 2 and Shali's part in it.

"I ... I do not know what to say." Shali paced the hardwood hallway. "How did you get my name and number?"

Emily filled her in on the mysterious events that guided the first Mission, and now this one. "That sound like a tale from a movie. How do I know what you tell me is real? Scams are everywhere these days."

The phone went quiet for a moment. *I guess I chase her away.* Shali started to push the 'off' button when Emily's voice came back softly.

"I agree with what you are saying, Shali, but all I have told you is true. I have experienced the arduous and sometimes dangerous process of the first Mission, and the almost heartbreaking events, while we searched for the document that led us to the second. I will not endeavor to convince you that what I have told you is right; you must make that choice yourself. If you need time to contemplate what I have told you, then do so. I can call you back."

"Okay, call me at the same time tomorrow," said Shali. "I need to consider this offer. Thank you." Emily acknowledged Shali and disconnected.

"Well, Pungu, I wanted my world to change, and maybe it is about to." Shali stroked her furry friend and then settled into a relaxing and thoughtful evening, exploring her new book.

19

MUNICH, GERMANY

While Halmar Fitzburg sat at the head of the large, mahogany table in the meeting room with four of his comrades, a knock sounded on the entry door. "Excuse me." He opened the door and took the note handed him. He sat again reading the message. A smile wrapped around his face.

"Well, gentlemen we have excellent news. Although Gavin and his comrades are in a Russian jail, they accomplished their mission to the letter. I will have to go to their 'hearing' next week. But I also have news that the devil stone was destroyed as we had planned. Those hellions have been defeated. They now know our power and are sure to give up their fruitless endeavors." He stood and held up a glass of water. "We have won." The other men stood and did likewise.

"General, why should they stop now?" Gedof asked. "Are there not more of those stones for them to find?"

The German smiled. "Yes, they may have more to find, but what we learned in their last mission two years ago, is they need all the stones for their insidious power to work. Without this one they are lost."

"But we are not sure how many stones are left?" Gedof pleaded.

The General smiled. "Ah, but we do. They need five more stones. Is not that correct, Kent?" Kent nodded. "They only finished one stone's completion. With this dead stone, the others are worthless."

A knock on the door alerted Fitzburg and he opened it. "Here it is comrades, what we have been waiting for – a message from our 'listeners' upstairs." He read the note that repeated what Greg had told Karl. "See? Even this man Greg knows they are finished."

"It is time for a celebration." He pulled a bottle of champagne from a cabinet behind his chair, and then passed it around the table. When everyone had a full glass, they stood, held up the glasses and shouted. "To victory, to Germany, to life!"

They sat for awhile chatting and enjoying their drinks, and then Fitzburg stood. "Now we have work to do. They still are teaching people false information. We must stop them. Tomorrow we make new plans to end these hellions' hold over our people."

20

JAVA

Emily talked with Shali, while Greg drove through an interesting volcanic chain of mountains in Java. As they enjoyed the drive through mountains, volcanoes, hills and valleys on their way to Borobudur, Greg joined the conversation.

"I have what you call 'ethnic diversity' in my family," Shali said, glancing at Greg while chatting with Emily. "My mother is Thai, and my father is French. So I am best of both worlds, they say."

Greg smiled. "I was curious what you do from a career standpoint."

"Thank you for asking." She laughed a little and continued. "I love flowers as a child, and I helped my mother in garden when we live near Bangkok. I expand it and bring exotic flowers from all over the world. This started my small business, when I am still in high school. I moved to Singapore, and attended business college. This is where I build my business. I own florist shops in Singapore, and other cities in Indonesia."

When Emily told Shali about their opponents, she replied. "Oh,

I am Indonesian Kung Fu black belt. We will show them a thing or two." And laughed.

They finally pulled into the parking area at the Borobudur Temple, and stretched their tired bodies.

"I am so excited about visiting temple," Shali said. "I always wanted to experience the eight terraces."

Greg closed the car door. "Me too, but I wonder if we'll really have time to do that and fully appreciate its significance. Time has become the critical factor and the faster the tenth Activation is completed, the better. We had to deal with The Cause a lot in the first Mission, but made it through on time. Recent delays with them continue to take time away from our Mission's completion date."

The temple looked even more impressive in person than the pictures Emily had seen. "I read that it had been covered in volcanic ash for centuries, and it wasn't until the early 1800's that an archeologist rediscovered its magnificence. Since that time, it has been completely dismantled and rebuilt, finished only recently." Emily turned her head upwards. "The ash had destroyed the temple's original white color; but it looks beautiful to me."

"The temple's five square, and three round terraces enabled 'pilgrims' to ascend along different layers. Each completed level represented a higher level of awareness, or the 'Eight-fold' path of Enlightenment, as it was called. Statues, carvings, and other elements guide the pilgrims through their initiations." Emily concluded.

Greg raised his eyebrows. "I haven't a clue where to begin, but we will know by tomorrow morning, and then we are off to work. We need to be careful about where we dig or disturb things."

The temple sat on a hill overlooking other ruins in the area. Nearby, Lorojanggrang — the priests' quarters at Borobudur — offered tantalizing areas to explore. While they studied the ruins, Greg took notes and made sketches of the complex so they could study it before starting their search. They also got a feel for the energy of the temple and other parts of the site. A working knowledge would contribute to shortening their search in the morning. Satisfied with their explorations, they found a hotel nearby, checked-in and met at the hotel restaurant.

Greg studied the steaming casserole. "I think we should start at the Temple and go from there. It might have secret areas that are below ground and were not disturbed by the ruined part" Greg brought a fork full of spicy tofu to his mouth.

"Something else. I read in guidebook: Lorojanggrang not as crowded, and not restored like temple," Shali said.

"Yeah, that is definitely where I want to explore in some depth away from the crowds; unless, of course we find access to your Stone around the Temple. The problem with poking around the Temple is the numbers of people who visit its terraces and roam about the grounds." Greg reached for the glass of red, Asian wine to soften the burning sensation in his mouth. "People at the top can see what's happening around the temple, and they might hinder our digging. We need a key, a clue of how to proceed. For now, we start at the temple, and then go to Lorojanggrang."

The next morning they entered the temple complex when it opened at six-thirty before many people arrived. They first explored the boundary of the temple for any signs of a possible hidden entrance. If ash had covered that whole area during the middle ages, then an adept would not have put a Stone inside the temple. But if the adept knew of a hidden entrance, he may have used it, ash or no.

After two hours of searching with no clues to follow, they moved on to the priest's quarters. The priests' quarters were truly in ruins. Greg couldn't discern their original structure, and therefore found it difficult to imagine where the adept would have hidden the Stone.

After an hour of searching, they took a break. "We need guidance," said Greg.

They formed a circle in the center of what resembled the remainder of a room within the priests' quarters, and held a short meditation. When they finished, they exchanged visions to assimilate their experiences.

"I saw rectangles that looked white, but had dirt over and around them keeping them partially hidden," said Greg.

Shali moved her hands in a long sweep in front of her. "My vision looked like a train; many boxcars moving down a track."

"Wow." Emily smiled. "I also saw white that seemed to move like one of those florescent signs pointing to something."

Greg moved his arm in a sweeping motion, while he talked. "We have white, a moving train, and a florescent sign pointing to something. So it would seem that our adepts formed a kind of arrow made of white, rectangular stones. Seems simple; just find a line of white stones." He smiled.

"I remember seeing some whitish stones," Emily said. "They were lying on the grass near the back of the most complete structure we've found so far."

They explored the ruins for a few minutes trying to locate the structure, when Greg almost tripped over some white rocks.

"There they are," Emily said, running over and almost knocking Greg down. "Let's follow their direction."

The three adventurers followed the rectangular stones, each about 30 mm long and almost buried in the dirt and grass, and came upon what looked like an old garden. It had an oblong shape from what they could vaguely see, with areas of tiny stone circles.

"These could have contained planted flowers, don't you think?" Emily surveyed the garden spotting other places like the patch in front of her.

The line of white stones ended at what could have been the center of a garden, just before a large white slab of rock half-buried. They cleared the covering with their shovels. While large, the stone looked movable, and they all grabbed one side and lifted. It fell on its top, revealing a stairway that looked well preserved.

Greg immediately descended the curved stairway, followed by the women. After about three meters and twelve steps, they reached the bottom of the stairs, and found an opening about a meter or so high in front of them. Each of them flashed their lights inside, revealing a tunnel. "Why a tunnel under a garden? Or had the garden been something else? A hiding place, maybe," Greg said.

Emily knelt and explored the tunnel with her light. "This looks manmade." The small tunnel forced them to remove their day-packs and pull them as they crawled at first until they arrived at a place about twenty meters inside where its height changed to about two meters. Even then, they still proceeded in a cramped, single-file, slow pace. It led downward toward the ruined buildings, leading Greg to believe it might have been used as an escape route. Along the way, he noticed braces for the ceiling about every 3 meters. It ended under one of the buildings Greg figured, when he noted what was left of a staircase to the right of the tunnel that must have once led up into a room. All they could see now were roots of foliage in a large earthen clump hanging from brown earth above them.

Greg shook his head. "Did our vision lead us to this and nothing else? There must be more than this"

"Of course there is more to it than 'this'." Emily filled the walls with light, flashing it everywhere. "We just need something called 'patience'."

They poked what was left of the walls with their small picks, looking for a sign to an entry that might lead them to the Stone. It appeared that earth had replaced the original staircase, covering all but a few steps at the bottom. The covered stairs looked like the only change that had taken place over a millennium. If there had been some other exit for the tunnel, earth had long ago covered it.

Greg put his hands on his hips and then sat on a stair. "Okay, let's see if we can come up with our next step. We come down some stairs hidden under a garden, make our way through a narrow tunnel, and arrive here at an earthen wall with an almost buried stairway on the right side of it." He pointed up the stairs. "Someone climbing the staircase doesn't make sense to me; if they had an entrance up there, why would they also have had the entrance we found?" He pointed to the earth wall at the end of the tunnel.

"If this tunnel continued, then it would go through there. What do you think?"

"It seem to me that the tunnel was built after stairway was covered." Shali said.

Emily shone her light up the stairway and dirt. "Yes, I agree. If they built the tunnel to hide from someone, the stairway up into a building would not have served them."

Greg got up. "So the question is *where* to start digging?" They nodded. "Okay, pick a place."

"Let's start here." Emily used her folding shovel to remove dirt from the wall in front of them next to the staircase. Taking turns, they had dug for about 30 minutes, when Shali's shovel sank beyond the wall. They stopped, and examined the dirt she removed. It differed from that in the walls of the tunnel with a lighter texture, and felt dryer. Had the dirt fallen from the ground above them into another hidden entrance just on the other side of the wall?

They dug faster, and soon the shape of a doorway emerged. "Looks like you made the right choice again Emily." Greg smiled.

They continued to dig into the entrance, and removed a broken brace of the original wooden arch. By now the little tunnel was half full of dirt. It wouldn't take much more dirt piled behind them to prevent them from getting out. They carefully piled shovelfuls of the dirt onto the stairs next to tunnel entry.

Then Emily's shovel broke through the wall into a void. It opened the top of what appeared to be a continuation of the tunnel, and they dug more dirt from it, being mindful of the dirt above them and its security from caving in. Soon they could see into a new tunnel. Before they proceeded, they spent an hour removing dirt. They emptied a daypack, filled it with dirt, and pulled it back out to the entryway and steps ten times.

Afterwards they crawled two meters through the now opened space to the new tunnel and then eased inside the opened entryway about two meters high. They then followed the tunnel for about 20 meters, slightly downward, where it stopped at a rotted, hanging door. Greg removed it to reveal a room that looked as if it had been undisturbed for ages. A large wooden dust covered table sat in the center, surrounded by chairs, and a series of wooden shelves lined the wall. Hidden behind cobwebs, dozens of books covered the shelves, as well as earthen vessels and an ancient smoking pipe.

Shali surveyed the shelves with intense interest. "I feel the Stone is near. I feel it."

"Yes, I think we've found the place we are looking for," Emily said. She removed a book and peeked behind it.

"Let's get to it, then," Greg said.

They used a cloth to clear the dust and cobwebs, and then removed everything from the shelves, and stacked the items on the table. A musty smell filled the room as dust fell from the books and cups. After emptying the shelves, Greg pulled on each shelf from the top, down, in an effort to loosen them from the brick wall. The shelves seemed to have been forced into a slot made with the bricks, while building the wall.

Meanwhile, Emily and Shali used their small picks on the spaces in between. When Greg pulled on the third shelf, it moved.

"Here, help me," Greg said, still holding the shelf.

Both women grabbed a part, and all three pulled at once. Falling backward when it came out of the wall, they dropped the shelf and scrambled to their feet. When the shelf came out of the wall, it not only left a space, but the section beneath it collapsed. A large hole, the width of the shelves, and about 20 millimeters deep, appeared behind the now vacant bookshelves. Inside, Greg's light revealed several leather sacks and small boxes.

"This must have been their 'safe,'" Greg said. As he reached inside, he felt a "buzz", the familiar energy of a Stone.

Emily and Shali simultaneously said, "I feel heat." They laughed.

They pulled out each sack and box, and laid them on the table. When they did, a faint light appeared within the cavity.

Greg didn't see it, but sensed the Stone's presence in a small box at the bottom of the hole when the 'buzz' started getting stronger. Light crept through the cracks and forced its way through every pore in the wood. While Shali removed the box, Emily pulled out a chair from the table, and Shali sat down.

She put the box in front of her, and slowly opened it. The energy seemed even more intense and a white light tinged with yellow, encircled her upper body and head. Shali's eyes widened, and her mouth opened. She sat there, transfixed for several minutes. Finally, Shali closed the box as carefully as she had opened it. They both stood beside her while she arose, clutching the box in both hands.

"I . . . I am most thrilled with this." She pulled the box to her heart. "You said it communicates with me in my mind. It did, just now. It said 'I love you.'"

They waited a few more minutes, feeling the energy and peace the Stone empowered within them. They explored the room a little more before leaving.

"These old books, those cups, all this stuff is priceless," Emily said. "I'd love to somehow get them to a museum." She sighed. "But, like all the rest we've seen, they remain buried until someone else finds them, I guess."

They looked for the hint of another doorway possibly hidden or covered by time. "If they made those passages, maybe they also created one to the temple." Greg peered up at the ceiling. Satisfied that there were no other ways out of the room, and they had nothing more to do there, they put everything back the best they could and left. They spent another hour finding their way back to the surface, and re-covering the hole to that part of the tunnel.

Emily let the sun caress her face. "It feels good to be back on the surface. It's way past lunch time and we've found the Stone. I think it's time to take a break."

They found a nearby restaurant, and collapsed in the sturdy metal chairs. Tired and hungry, they needed to relax. After ordering, Greg and Emily talked with Shali about what she might expect from the Stone.

"Until now, we've always found a Stone late in the day," Emily said. "And the Recipient had all night to communicate with it.

But now, we've got plenty of daylight left, and we could look for the Activation site."

Greg interrupted. "Not until Shali has thoroughly communicated with her Stone. We could be chasing our tails without the right information."

"Yes, of course. I didn't mean to just go out and wing it." Emily said.

"Why don't you take the Stone to a quiet, private place, and meditate with it for awhile? Then we can follow whatever guidance you get. If it leads us to the Activation Site, and you are guided to proceed, we do it. If not, then we wait."

Shali turned her eyes up, then down as if considering the proposition. "Yes. I see what you mean. I will try it."

After finishing the quick, but satisfying meal they left the restaurant, and found a secluded area of the park. The temple and other ruins were located in an Archeological Park with plenty of greenery. They found a comfortable area to sit and enjoy the surroundings. Emily and Greg picked a spot away from Shali to give her whatever privacy she needed. Greg lay on the soft grass and watched some puffy, white clouds change shape. Many times he had turned to the sky for messages from Spirit. The cloud shapes, and sometimes colors, always spoke to him, giving him direction. Soon they formed into a pyramid-looking shape, which he interpreted to mean the temple. That changed to what looked like a doorway that first opened, and then closed. The cloud then rapidly evaporated.

Puzzled, he passed on a description of the scene to Emily. "I saw visions of the shape of a temple, and then a door that opened and closed."

Emily glanced at the sky. "That surely is a sign that I think we can count on to begin our search. Of course, there are plenty of temples to pick from."

Greg touched her hand. "Since it is getting later in the day, could it mean to start our exploration for the Site, but go no further than that discovery?"

"Of course," said Emily. "Find an entrance to it, and then leave its exploration for tomorrow."

They resumed their relaxation, eyes closed, waiting for Shali. Greg drifted off into another world of light and rainbows, flying on golden-white clouds. He landed in a fairy-tale town, with castles disappearing into the sky. He was about to enter one, when he heard a voice call his name. Greg looked for the owner within the mystical world, when he suddenly realized the voice was Shali's. He opened his eyes, and she stood above him. He got up, searching for Emily, but found her gone.

Confused, he turned to Shali. "Have you seen Emily?"

"No. I come over here and saw you sleep."

They searched the area, Greg running at times, checking every direction. He couldn't have slept more than five or ten minutes, before Shali called him. Where could Emily have gone that quickly? Panicky thoughts raced through his mind, and visions of big brutes abducting her played like scenes from a movie.

When Greg started toward the car, he noticed a familiar figure strolling toward the spot where he and Emily had lain side by side. He shouted "Emily?!" and ran toward the figure. He reached for her shoulder and almost fell against her. She quickly turned and moved aside, pushing him away.

"Greg! What are you doing?" She gave him a wild stare. "You startled me. Where did you come from?"

"Where did *I* come from? Where did *you* come from? I woke up and you were gone. I thought you had been abducted." She laughed and he could feel his face getting red, and his muscles tighten.

"Abducted? Why would someone kidnap me in the middle of a park full of people? You have a great imagination, my darling. I went to the Ladies Room while you snoozed. Maybe I should tie a rope around my leg so you could reel me in whenever I am missing." She laughed again, and then threw her arms around him. At first, he resisted, and then melted into her embrace. "Let go of what happened in Bhutan. Terkenni is behind bars."

They sat on the grass, while Shali explained what she had learned from her meditation experience. "There is another entry at priests' quarters, but nearer the temple. It lead to underground chamber, maybe goes beneath temple."

Emily checked her watch. "We don't have enough time to find the entrance and perform the ceremony before sunset. But maybe we do have enough time to at least find the entrance." She glanced at Greg. "Just like your vision."

Greg remembered his cloud experience. *What a confirmation.*

They went back to the priests' quarters to search in an area they hadn't previously explored. While they surveyed the grounds, Greg noticed that the building looked as if it had exploded. Parts of it lay about a central foundation, so they probed the debris as a place to start.

Shali wandered off toward the temple, and as Greg watched, she suddenly disappeared. Shouting her name, Greg ran over to where he had last seen her, and almost fell into a huge depression in the ground. He reached down and helped her up as Emily arrived.

"Look," said Emily. "That depression looks as though a large stone was once here."

Greg pointed. "It must have fallen from the building, and then have been removed; but it does give us a possibility of finding an entry to our Activation place. 'There are no accidents'."

They scrutinized the surrounding area and inside the cavity for the sign of an entrance.

"Let us ask if this is right place." Shali stared at the cavity.

Emily and Gregg nodded, and then sat across from Shali who was already seated. After ten minutes of silence, Shali arose.

"We are here. Below is the way to Activation site." She removed a shovel from her pack, jumped into the hole and dug in the center.

Within minutes, her shovel broke through the soft dirt into space. Using his light, Greg found signs of a tunnel below the cavity. All three dug out more dirt, and then Shali jumped into what looked like a tunnel.

"I explore the tunnel a little," she said. "Hand me a light."

She was gone for a few minutes. When she returned, Greg helped her out of the hole. "It look like a tunnel that goes toward temple. I think we find entry to Activation Site."

They covered the hole with surrounding debris of branches and held them in place with a large rock, and then left. Greg stopped at the reception area of the complex to check for mail. He was given two boxes. "The phones have arrived," he said to Emily when she met him at the door. "We need to call Karl as soon as we get to the hotel room."

21

SEDONA, AZ

K arl Josephon sat quietly and studied the notebook. *The Arizona
sun rose softly above red rocks, spilling hues of red across the
landscape. His brief talk with Emily the previous evening gave
him confidence that their plan was working. They had decided
that Emily and Greg would stay in the field and only call Karl
once a week, or in an emergency, from their encrypted phone. Karl
could not call them as his phone could only receive. The only way
Karl could reach them was through Shannon, as she had the only
"call out" phone, which was also enciphered.

Karl noticed that his cup was empty, poured more hot coffee
and sat back in the chair staring at a picture of Emily, Greg, and
himself displayed on the table across from him.

He missed those two, but it was a wise choice that they stay
away from Sedona. He took his cup of coffee to his lounger and
enjoyed the morning. Since the next site to visit was only revealed
at the conclusion of the present Wisdom Stone's Activation, even
Greg and Emily did not know the next place to go until then. Karl
smiled. *If only this system had been in place last time, those scoundrels*

wouldn't have caused so much trouble. He got up and moved to the kitchen, where he made some eggs.

After eating, Karl carried his cup to his small, round work table where the course manual lay. It was time to finish studying this and get ready for next week's class. He drank some coffee, while flipping through the manual, sat back and twirled a pencil between his fingers bouncing it against the table top. He also had to get ready to go north again and help Jasmine at Mt. Shasta. A knock on the front door of his condo interrupted his contemplation.

Karl greeted three men. "May I help you?"

The largest, muscular man said, "Yes you may." And stepped into the condo past Karl. The other two followed.

"I am Gedof, and I smell coffee. Get us some." He and the others sat at the kitchen table.

"Wha' ... what do you want?" Karl said. "Get out of my house, now."

Gedof gave him an evil smile. "We want knowledge. And you have that knowledge Mr. Josephon. Come join us for a chat."

Karl stood at the table, his hands on his hips. "Just who the hell are you?"

"We are the people who have been trying to stop you and your comrades from spreading your evil work." Gedof held a smirk. "You already know our leader, General Fitzburg."

Karl gave him a puzzled look. "What do you expect me to tell you?"

"We have been watching your place and the other two for the past two days." Gedof said, "We want to know where your friend, Greg and his pretty girlfriend are so we can all sit down and discuss closing your classrooms."

Karl grimaced. "They are on their way back here, thanks to you."

Gedof grabbed Karl's neck. "Really? Did they take a 'round the world trip' to get here?"

"What's it to you?" Karl coughed. "Greg said he would get back to me, or just show up."

The German let go of Karl's throat. "Bostone, Pilgroy, search the house. Find anything you can about where these people may be doing their dirty work." Gedof stood over Karl.

Karl didn't know what else to do. He faced three men, most likely carrying weapons, and could not expect to accomplish any kind of defensive action.

The men began going through the desk, files cabinets, drawers, and anywhere else that might contain the information they sought.

An hour later they reported back to Gedof. "Nothing. This place has nothing about their location."

"How 'bout you call them?" Gedof handed him the phone.

Karl wasn't sure what to do. Emily and Greg in Java would probably only answer the enciphered phone he had sent to Shannon. Other than letting the three know about the other phone in a closet, this seemed to be his only out. So he dialed. As expected, there was no answer. "He evidently has the phone turned off. My friend, Shannon has Emily's number on her phone. Why don't I call her and have her call Emily?"

"You trying to tell me you do not have this Emily's number? How would you have one and not the other?" Gedof gave him an angry look.

Karl frowned. "She lost her phone and had to get a new one with a new number. I don't have it yet, but Shannon does, because the two talked right after the change."

"Okay, call." Gedof said. "But no funny business."

Karl dialed the number. "Hi Shannon. I need a quick favor. Could you call Emily and find out where they are and when they expect to get back? I don't have her number and can't reach Greg. I really need them back here as soon as possible."

Shannon paused. "Ah, okay. I'll call you back. My phone is in the car." Shannon clicked her phone off. Realizing something was up, she dialed out on the enciphered phone. She talked to Greg and told him about the strange call from Karl. Greg agreed to call Karl right away on Karl's regular phone.

Karl hung up. "She or one of the other two will call me right back."

Gedof leaned back in the chair. "Okay, we wait. But not for long."

Karl's phone rang. "Hi Karl, Greg. What's up?"

"You need to drop whatever you are doing and get back here right away." Karl said. "I have three men here who want to talk with us about closing our classrooms. So your presence is needed soon."

Karl repeated to Gedof. "Greg said he would finish up what they were doing and be on the next flight back here promptly. Okay?"

"Tell him *soon*. We will not wait long, before we use other measures to get what we want." Karl repeated the message to Greg. He agreed and disconnected.

"So we wait." Gedof stood. "One of my men will stay here and keep us informed. Meanwhile, I will be in touch with our leader and let him know what is going on." The three men stepped outside for a moment, and then Pilgroy returned. "Continue what you were doing. I will just hang around and be sure you behave yourself."

Karl took a deep breath. *I need to be careful. Lord knows what this guy is capable of.*

22

JAVA, INDONESIA

The rising sun peeked through windows of the large hotel room. Its golden rays struck a crystal decoration overhead and reflected onto several tables. Emily and Shali discussed her communication with the yellow Stone, during breakfast.

"It told me to bring two Earth elements for the Activation Ceremony," Shali said. "A leaf from a Banyan tree and stem of white, lace-like flowers."

Emily put her fork down on the empty plate. "With all of the greenery surrounding the temples, that should be easy."

"I hope so." Shali picked up her coffee cup with both hands and sipped the hot liquid.

Greg joined the conversation. "We seem to have plenty of time to find the Activation site before sunset, but even so we can't slow down either. Even though finding that entrance yesterday gave us a measure of time, we never know what we're up against." He pushed the last piece of egg covered English muffin onto his fork. "Of course, we have to fold in the possibility of our assailants showing up. Although I feel we have that taken care of, at least for this trip."

"I agree," said Emily and glanced at Shali. "We must be ever vigilant today." Shali nodded. "On a lighter note: do you realize this is the first time anyone has ever found the way to a site the same day as finding the Stone?"

Greg held up his cup. "To the first time; and to a great today." They all laughed and clinked their cups together.

They left the restaurant, picked up their packs, and drove to the temple parking area. All three carefully scrutinized the area after they arrived at the site. Seeing nothing unusual, German scoundrels lurking about for instance, they enjoyed the perfect morning with its blue sky, bright, warm sunshine, singing birds and beautiful surroundings – a "hanging out" kind of day. But they had a job to do, and time became more critical with each passing moment. After all, they still had two more Stones to find and activate by November 11th, only a month away.

Since they needed to gather the earth elements before entering the tunnel, they combed the grounds first. Shali searched for a Banyan tree to find the leaves she needed. Meanwhile, Emily and Greg hunted for the flower Shali had described during breakfast.

Many flowers grew in the park, which covered a large area.

Emily swept her hand across the field. "When we find the flower, I will take several pieces, and break them off at the ground. That way, Shali can remove the parts she needs, and discard the lower parts containing my energy."

Greg let Emily do most of the searching, while he kept Shali in sight. Since the Recipient was the most important person in the Activation scenario, and *she had the Stone,* he wanted to assure her safety. Maybe he was getting paranoid, which made no sense because both women were expert martial arts practitioners. However, after their experience in Bhutan, he knew that even people with better skills than theirs can get in big trouble with ruthless terrorists.

Emily circled the field amazed at the multitude of flowers; such beautiful flowers. She could pick a bundle of them and take them to the hotel with her. But that would not work right now.

Her search continued among red, green, violet, and other shades of finely shaped blossoms. "Ah, there you are." She bent down and scooped up a couple of the desired blossoms, careful to only touch the bottoms.

Joyful she found her prize, and holding a stem of flowers she skipped back to where Greg stood. "Ah so you have found the required flowers?" Greg asked.

"Yes indeed. Let's show Shali." Said Emily.

When they approached Shali her face lit up. "Yes, they are the ones I saw in my vision. Thank you. I am not being lucky in finding my leaf." Shali circled the tree, and they followed. A whole grove of trees stood in front of her, and then she stopped. "Here, this is it." Shali pulled a low branch to her. She then pulled off a hand-full of leaves, and examined them. "I now have the two elements. You bring me luck Emily." Shali took what she needed from the flower stems, and put them and the leaves in a bag she had brought from the hotel, careful not to crush them.

They moved on to the tunnel. Checking that no one watched them, they slid the covering back just enough to allow access to the small hole. Greg helped the two women into the tunnel, and then threw them the packs. He turned and visually swept his surroundings carefully, then jumped into the hole. From inside the one meter wide, dirt tunnel with a shored up meter and a half high ceiling, they quickly maneuvered the rock over the hole. Satisfied they were unseen, and now hidden within a mysterious tunnel, they moved on.

They continued slightly downward, for a hundred meters and then noticed it getting narrower, the opposite of what they had normally seen. "This is different," said Greg. "But it is hand-dug and not a natural cave so it doesn't surprise me."

The ceiling then got lower and they had to proceed in a "bent over" position for awhile, before the tunnel opened into a larger room-like area. Again, it looked manmade. "This place could have been some kind of assembling area before entering the main hall, or a hiding place." Emily said.

They searched the 'room' for an exit of some kind. Spying an odd-looking, door-like appendage on the wall opposite the tunnel, they examined the structure. It resembled a metal shield, with an axe on both sides and a broadsword at the bottom. It seemed to be attached to an almost hidden door. Greg pulled on the hardware, but it didn't move.

"This looks to me like a possible door opening," said Greg. "Maybe I can make it work using one of these attachments." Greg took one of the axes from the configuration. He pushed the blade behind the shield, and pried it out with the axe handle. The shield moved a little.

Emily peered over his shoulder. "I would be careful with that relic. We don't want to destroy our ancestors' work of art."

"I hear you, but we have to do something to get beyond here." Then he spotted two pegs attached to the shield protruding into the wall, evidently impeding his progress. He repeated his effort with the axe three more times before the shield yielded. He then banged it the rest of the way out with the axe blade.

"Taking out your frustrations, are you?" Emily smiled and stepped back.

Greg shot her a wry smile and crawled into a small hole behind the fallen shield. It just fit his body, so he removed his pack before proceeding. He used his flashlight, and crawled 20 meters before coming to a small room. It contained remnants of water jugs, and other vessels. It looked like a hiding place for the previous occupants, but maybe a dead end for entrance to an Activation Site. He crawled back out, and reported his findings. "It may have potential, but I think we need to search further."

All three swept the walls with their lights and found two other shields. Greg wondered whether they were decoys, or hid other rooms. So he repeated his prying techniques on the other two shields and found two more small rooms.

Ignoring the new rooms, Greg crawled back out to the large room. "What purpose did these rooms serve?" He scratched his head, thinking aloud.

"If they served as hiding places, why the pegs dug into the earth?" Emily said, staring into the last hole he uncovered "How would they have closed them from the inside? Maybe they hid some-*thing*, but not themselves,"

"The earth too symmetric, unnatural. We need to find natural place," Shali pointed out.

"Yes, of course. You had described a natural place from your vision. But that doesn't preclude traversing an *unnatural place* to get to it. These look like dead-ends, but we have run into roadblocks before, and found ways through them. Greg glanced at the three uncovered areas "Maybe we are on the right track, and maybe not."

"Why did they go down?" Emily said.

Greg faced her with a puzzled stare. "What?"

"Why did they go down?" Emily stared at the tunnel "Why would they have dug down, just to provide a hiding place? Staying on the same level would have served the same purpose. There must be some reason for the tunnel to suddenly drop six meters in elevation."

Greg glanced at her, startled at her sudden revelation and keen observation.

"Amazingly astute, my dear. If they went down, then it must have been to get below something . . . like the temple." He pulled out his notepad. "According to my scribbles, we have come about 200 meters. I would estimate that the temple is right above us. If that's so, then there must be a way of getting to it. What do you think?"

"I don't know, but the temple being above us makes sense to me," said Emily.

"Stone says 'go up'." Shali had one hand on the sack containing the Stone, which she had tied around her neck, and the other hand pointing straight up.

"Right. Ask it *how?*" Greg said, "because going up doesn't look feasible from here."

"Through the door," came Shali's answer he hadn't expected. His question had been rhetorical.

"Anything else?"

"No." Shali said.

"Through the door." Greg quizzically spun around searching as did the other two. Was there another door here or one in the other rooms? Either the 'shielded' rooms served a purpose, or they were decoys. Emily and Shali jabbed their small picks in the wall, while Greg examined the areas around the once-shielded holes. He crawled back into one of them to take a closer look. Could there be a hidden doorway? He examined the walls closely. They seemed flawless, not a trace of anything remotely resembling an entrance. *Why search only the walls? Why not the floor?* He stomped the floor with his foot and listened for hollow sounds.

He repeated his efforts in the other rooms, while the women continued to examine the larger room. Halfway finished in the third room, he heard a scream. He quickly crawled out to where Emily and Shali yelled.

"What's going on?"

"Look, there's a door here." Emily pointed to the wall in front of her. "Shali was chipping down there, and I was here, and poof the door slid open a crack."

"Way to go. You've solved the mystery." He pushed his shovel into the crack and pried the door open. "Very clever. A work of art. It matches the wall perfectly. Its joints look precision made. There must be some point, or points, that when pressed opened it. Only the priests knew where to do that, so it was safely concealed."

They made their way into the new corridor, the largest of all the ones they had visited. The tunnel went straight for about ten meters then spiraled upward. It ended in another large room. This one looked natural and much larger than the others. Altars stood like forgotten relics in a museum, dust covering every inch of their silver surfaces. Sacred artifacts lay everywhere. At one end, a huge pile of dirt rose above the altars and seemed to come from the wall. Close inspection revealed a doorway that probably led to stairs and a way up to the temple.

They knew they had found the Activation site, and Shali could begin the ceremony. With almost two hours until sunset, they decided to eat a snack of pita bread with cheese and some mangos, and have some chai tea for the lunch they had not yet eaten. "Is this temple liable to be uncovered in future?" Shali asked. "Yellow Stone need safety from intruders."

"Hmm, never thought of that." Emily glanced at Greg.

He acknowledged Emily's intriguing look "While that is possible, I doubt we would have been led here if this were so. We need to trust that this is the right place."

"I agree. I just wanted to get your input." Emily smiled.

During their snack time, Emily noted the arrangement of the altars in the room. There were six total with the largest one at the center of the others and somewhat taller. She surmised that it would be the one used for the Activation.

Afterwards, they put their equipment away and stood by to help Shali in whatever way she asked them, while she prepared for, and performed the Activation ceremony. Standing back and shining her light on the alters, Emily noticed a symmetrical design - five altars stood about 3 meters apart in a semi-circle, while the tall altar stood at the center of the semi-circle and up 2 meters from the first two. The pattern comprised about two thirds of the room.

Shali stepped to the center altar and wiped it clean using water from her jug. She then took the sack from around her neck, removed the little wooden box, and laid it on the altar. She opened the box and slid the top back. The Yellow colored Stone, shaped like a star, radiated light and soft energy. She held the Stone to her heart. "I feel love, like I am floating in light." With both hands she placed it on the altar. When she did, a glow, beyond what she described earlier, radiated softly from the Stone, and grew brighter with each breath she took.

When its brightness lit the room, a figure emerged suspended above it. The figure took near-human form and spread its 'arms' around the three of them. Greg felt warmth, harmony and heartfelt love that filled the depth of his being and every cell in his body. He also knew things that it would be impossible to put into words. Not only did he have knowledge about the human condition and the relationship with Spirit, but he felt also that he could use it wisely.

Emily closed her eyes as the 'arms' seemed to melt into her body. She felt love similar to when she was in Machu Picchu witnessing the Activation of the Green Stone. A warm glow seemed to soothe her body.

The figure spoke. "Blessings to one and all. I am Belienna. I come to you from a realm of wise and gentle souls that wish you well. We have waited for this event for millennia and are joyous at its coming. This beautiful Stone brings Vision to you and your world. Shall we begin?"

"Shali, please take the leaves, crumble them and place them at the center of this altar." She did so. "Now place the Stone upon the bed of leaves and sing with me."

Shali gently placed the Stone as instructed and stepped back from the altar. A beautiful and joyful voice sang blessings to the Stone, while the three joined Belienna and shared the joy. It sounded like a mantra, a chant and melodious song all at once. Music filled the room, accompanying their voices, and harmony spread throughout. Greg turned trying to identify where the music originated and its instruments, but saw nothing. Belienna's arms waved rhythmically with the music. The singing lasted for about ten minutes, and then faded as did their voices, in unison with it.

Belienna embraced them again. "Shali, please take the flower petals and drop them over the Stone" Again she followed Belienna's instructions, releasing a handful of petals, like snowflakes, onto the Stone.

Belienna spoke again. "The leaves and petals come from the Earth, and this Stone honors Her fullness and completeness regarding the natural beauty you call Nature. Each Stone you dedicated servants have Activated blesses the Earth, and joyously enters into Earth's energy field and shares Her joy. Upon completion of the twelfth Activation and the Winter Solstice, all Stones will join, combining their energy and enfold the Earth with it. Each human upon the planet will feel that energetic shift and choose whether to ride with it, or ignore it."

Belienna then moved about the room arranging the remaining altars in a circle around the one containing the Yellow Stone. When she finished, five additional altars glistened in the Stone's radiance.

Upon returning to the center, Belienna moved her hands over the altar as if weaving. Soon, a tapestry unfolded from her handiwork and hung in the room above the altar, like the moon hangs above the earth. A yellow background highlighted a woven picture of the earth with twelve stones surrounding it.

"Let us dance," Belienna said and moved to the first of the five altars surrounding the Stone. When she did, a mixture of sand, clay and other earthen elements covered it, representing the first element —Earth. Music resounded throughout the room again and they danced to it.

Belienna moved to the second altar and Air spiraled upward from it representing the second element.

She moved to the third altar and Water flowed from it, representing the third element. They continued dancing while the music changed its tempo and melody with each element change.

She moved to the fourth altar and Fire sprang from it, representing the fourth element.

Finally she moved to the last altar, and a tree rose from its center, representing Wood – the fifth element. The music reached a crescendo, and then slowly faded. The dancers also stopped their dancing and then sat before the altars.

Belienna moved to the center altar and hung above it. A soft yellow column of light flowed from the Temple above to the Yellow Stone when she spoke.

"This Stone brings forth the Yellow Ray. This Ray symbolizes and focuses on mental power and vision, but also joy. It gives humans the ability to find solutions through use of cosmic wisdom, rather than the human intellect. By focusing on the Yellow Ray and feeling its spiritual power within when problem solving, humans will benefit greatly. Use it also when feeling depressed: visualize this Ray bathing

you in its joyful light. It will lift your consciousness and help you cre-
ate a virtuous perspective when dealing with others. Acting from this
perspective and from the joy inspired by the Yellow Ray will result in
compassionate service. Order and discretion will be your daily attri-
butes as you move out into the world joyfully serving through spiritu-
ally motivated vision.

The visionary looks not backward at what might have been, but
eternally forward at what can be. It is with great Vision that ancient
Prophets and Masters have foretold what was to come. The Master
Jesus said: 'These things that I do, you also can do . . . and even more.'
Did he not give you the Secret, in just that one sentence? Your Vision is
your life. Without it you crumble as clay when it dries. Wet clay can be
molded, forming the vision held within the molder's heart." Belienna
moved her hands simulating the molding process.

"How joyful it is to know that at the center of your Being is The
One, or God in human terms. From that center all things are done, all
words are spoken, and all thoughts manifest. Joy lifts you to the highest
state of being, from which you move out into your world. It is bringing
the Within to the without that allows joy to embrace all that you do.
It is a motivator, an inspiration to do more and lift the doing to new
heights. It changes your perspective of whatever is happening in your
life so that it is seen through the eyes of God."

Belienna fell silent while she focused on the Stone and the
elements around it. A rainbow formed around the altar and the
whole room vibrated. A wave of light emerged that went through
Shali like a lightening bolt, yet she said that its essence felt loving,
joyous, and peaceful. They all sat and waited while the ever-in-
creasing energy flooded the room and moved out through the
solid walls.

Belienna then stood before them and placed her hands on each
of their heads. Greg felt peace like he had never known, and the
realization of "Who I truly Am." He felt a Presence within and
knew it as his Higher Self supporting and loving him, with love
that could not be described. He watched the others and felt that
they experienced the same kind of Presence as well.

There was silence. The room vibrated, and light moved with the vibration. A feeling of love moved within Emily and the others so powerful that tears flowed like water from a fountain. Each moved to the tapestry and each wiped their tears upon it, bowing as they did so.

Belienna's image encompassed all of the altars, and they backed away when she said, "It is finished." Her image remained like a halo around the Stone's altar.

As they quietly left the room, each in deep thought, Emily received a message in her mind from Belienna. "I have a message for you Emily. I am to tell you that your next activation site is Chichen Itza in Mexico." They made their way back down the ramp. When they reached the smaller room, they pressed the right places around the door and it vanished. Only a wall remained.

"It looks like your Stone is safe, Shali," said Emily. "There is only a wall to see right now."

They moved back up the tunnel toward the 'entry' hole, but on the way Greg stopped. "We need a way close this tunnel in case someone stumbles onto it. Let's look for a way to pull down the some of the ceiling struts."

"I suggest we do that close to the entrance lest we get trapped in the cave in." Emily scanned the ceiling and the struts holding it.

Greg did the same. "Yes, I agree."

They soon found a 'trigger' and Greg carefully engaged it after the women stood at the entrance. A small 'earthquake' closed the tunnel to the room leaving only dirt for an inquiring visitor to see. After leaving the hole, they maneuvered the large rock they used earlier to collapse into it, closing the hole and sealing it.

Greg and Emily had just returned to their hotel room, when the enciphered phone sounded. After finishing the call from Karl, Greg explained to Emily what just happened. "We need to go back to Sedona and meet with those men, and also make adjustments.

Emily gave him a concerned look. "What are we going to do? Once we get back to Sedona, we will be watched. How are we going to get to the next site?"

"I don't know right now, but we will find an answer."

While getting ready for their evening meal, Emily let Greg know what Belienna had given her about the next site. Mexico will be a lot closer to home, Greg thought.

The three adventurers met in the hotel's dinning hall, and ordered scrumptious local Javanese meals for their final time together, and discussed the Stone's message.

"You know, there doesn't seem to be much in the way of a vision in the minds of people today. Most of us live our daily lives without seeking a better way." Greg mused, as he cut a piece of jackfruit boiled in coconut oil.

Emily sipped some egg stew. "I always thought of a vision as something a guru sees for humanity, but I get that a vision can be about anything. The chief executive of a company sees a vision of where it is going, and takes the steps to get them there. Anyone can have a vision; it is the purpose of the vision that is important."

"That a mouthful," Shali said. They all laughed.

Greg sliced through a piece of babat cake with his fork. "Yes, I think most of us take an everyday vision for granted as we move through life. Since not many of us have really witnessed a sacred vision like we just experienced, it is difficult to describe, and integrate into our lives."

"Maybe we need to look inside us for our true vision," Shali said grabbing a piece of spring roll.

Emily and Greg smiled, and nodded. But in the back of their minds they knew they needed to change their plans and get to Sedona first thing in the morning. The threat loomed of The Cause hurting Karl, and bashing their plans for Mexico.

23

SEDONA, AZ

torm clouds rolled into the Arizona sky, turning mid-day into dusk. Thunder shook Karl's condo, startling its unwelcome occupant of two days. The condo's usually neat appearance suffered from the behavior of his "guest" waiting for a phone call. Karl was coerced to provided food and drink as Pilgroy entertained himself in the den with TV and movies.

While Karl attempted to study the lessons for the next class, the phone rang. "Hi Karl, we're at the airport. Can you come pick us up?" Greg said.

"Let me ask my 'guard'." Karl replied. "Pilgroy, the people you have been waiting for are at the airport. I need to go get them and bring them here. Is it okay if I stop at their homes so they can cleanup and change first?"

Pilgroy stood. "You think I am a fool? I will accompany you. But first I will call Gedof." The man got his comrade on the phone and explained the situation. "Sure, go ahead. We will meet you at Karl's." Pilgroy put on his gun and coat, and then they left for the airport.

When they arrived, Emily and Greg put their luggage in the trunk. When they entered the car, each gave Pilgroy, sitting in the backseat, a surprised look.

"For a minute, I wondered if you had become a chauffeur, Karl." Greg eyed the intruder.

Pilgroy pulled out his gun, holding it low near the seat. "One of you get back here with me."

Greg complied. "Home, James." He smiled.

They all grew quiet for a few minutes, when Greg leaned forward. "Well we are in quite a messy situation right now, aren't we Karl?"

Karl nodded. "We also need to decide about this 'closing the classrooms' thing."

"That's not going to happen," said Emily. "We will have to work something out with these guys."

Pilgroy interrupted. "You might as well save your breath, until we get back to Karl's. Gedof will meet us there to spell out demands. Then you can have your say."

Thirty minutes later they arrived at Karl's condo. Waiting for them were the other two men. Once inside, Karl made some tea and they sat around the dining room table to talk.

"General Fitzburg discussed your situation with all of us." Gedof wore a smile. "Since you have lost the ability to complete your mission, which we so expertly engineered, you still are teaching people false ways of living. We cannot let that continue. So all we ask is that you step down from your pedestals and find other employment."

Emily leaned forward. "You and your general must have realized when you made plans to come here that we would refuse to do that. Since you have destroyed the energy that helps support our efforts to teach, the school will eventually die anyway. So why don't you just leave us alone and let us live with our defeat."

"Well said, Emily." Gedof responded. "However, we see it differently. Whether you eventually stop teaching is not the issue. We want it to stop now. We were not sent here to bargain with you. We came here to stop you."

Greg frowned. "And how do you propose doing that?"

"There are ways." Gedof said. "Let's see; we could blow up more classrooms, kidnap someone, wreak havoc on your students. Shall I continue?"

Greg and Emily stood. "We are finished. You can leave now and tell your leader that we will continue teaching. End of meeting." They turned and moved to the front door.

"You go out that door and your friend here will suffer the consequences." Gedof put his hand on Karl's shoulder.

Emily and Greg turned and grabbed Karl. "Then we will take him with us."

The three men pulled out their guns and moved toward Karl, Emily, and Greg. Emily glanced at Greg and then she ducked, swirled, and kicked Pilroy's legs out from under him. At the same time, Greg turned toward Gedof planting the heel of his foot in the man's gut. When Gedof bent over from the kick, Greg grabbed the gun and then brought the handle down across Gedof's head.

Meanwhile, Emily had floored Pilgroy whose gun went flying across the room.

The third man, Bostone, looked surprised at the sudden outburst from Emily and Greg, and pushed his gun into Karl's back. Karl hit the floor, rolled over, and caught Bostone's groin with his foot. He then got up and grabbed the gun, while the man bent over in pain. He then ran to the bathroom and dialed 911.

Meanwhile, Greg and Emily kept the men covered, and asked Karl to find something to tie them with. He produced some twine, which he and Emily used to tie the men's arms behind their backs. Ten minutes later the police arrived, while Greg and Emily were still trying to secure the three men. Karl charged them with kidnapping, harassment, and assault.

"We've bought some time," said Emily. "But they will be back."

Greg put his arms around both of them. "Let's take a walk."

They gave him a quizzical look, but caught on to what he meant. Once outside and strolling amongst the Red Rocks a few minutes later, Greg continued. "We need to monitor our conversations, and we have some Stones to find and Activate. Here is what I propose. Emily stays here and I will go to Mexico to meet our next Recipient. That way they won't get suspicious of Emily and me leaving here so quickly. And … here is an even better idea. Since we now have two objectives, one, to find and activate two more Stones, and two, keep the classes going, we need more people actively participating."

Greg pulled out a pad and pencil. "We have two more sites to visit, but also must show our faces here. I take Shannon's classroom guard, Isabel, with me to Mexico and train her to do what you do, Emily. Then, we send Shannon and Isabel to the final site."

"Wow, you have really gotten serious with this 'looking as though you are here, but really setting things up for Activations' facade." Emily smiled. "I say go for it."

"Sounds like a good idea," said Karl. "Emily can take over what I have been doing, and I can get back to the finance aspect of our company." They all agreed that Greg would use the enciphered phones and come back after the activation. That way he would not be gone too long. "Emily can say I am taking a vacation or visiting another office or something."

Emily smiled. "Go for it, my love. Once we get the last two sites activated the energy will change, and maybe our German friends won't be so nasty."

The next day, Greg left for Chichen Itza.

24

TELA, HONDURAS

he normally blue sky over Tela, Honduras grew dark, while Carlos snorkeled through the clear water nearby. He glanced up and noticed drops piercing the water's top. *Time to leave. A storm is coming.* He surfaced, took off his gear and sprinted to his bike. A beach is nowhere to hang out during a thunderstorm, he knew from experience. He had seen a friend struck by lightening when he was young. The boy lived but had terrible dreams, and hid whenever a storm approached.

Carlos reached his house just as the rain grew heavy and the lightening increased. He pushed the bike into the back of the carport and dashed into the bungalow. "Ah, I am safe and in time for food." Carlos tossed his gear in the hall closet and hugged his wife, Darsella.

"You have learned to come in from the rain," she said. "Almost as smart as Spooky." She smiled, and leaned down and patted their black lab's head.

After lunch, the rain still pelted the tile roof and windows. "What will you do now, on your day off? You cannot snorkel in the rain."

Carlos sighed. "I guess I will read my book. Or," he moved closer to his wife on the sofa, "I make love to you." He put his arms around her. Spooky put his paws up on the sofa and his nose near theirs. "Ah, Spooky, you are such a spoiler."

The rain stopped two hours later, but by then it was too late to resume his venture under the water. "The sea will wait for another day, my love." Carlos turned from the window and pulled Darsella close. "But I have more time with you."

They spent the rest of the evening together: eating supper and enjoying music, with Carlos playing along on his guitar.

The next day at his job as district manager for one of Honduras's seafood companies, Carlos got a call from his wife. "Someone named Emily? What did she want? Sounds crazy. Yes, I will return home by six." He put the phone down with a perplexed look. What would a woman from the United States want with him? It was puzzling.

Carlos met with several buyers from the United States during the day, causing him to consider the phone call even more. At lunch with some friends, Carlos mentioned the mysterious phone call. "Ah, Carlos is sought by beautiful women even as far away as the United States. What does Darsella think of this?" said Prenta. They all laughed.

The phone rang within ten minutes, after Carlos returned home that evening. "Yes, this is Carlos, how can I help you?" Emily explained who she was and why she had called. "You call to joke with me, right? I do not know what you talk about." As usual, Emily related details, information about the Mission, and why it was so important.

"You do not make joke then. What you tell me is real." Carlos had a pensive look. "I must consider this undertaking. Call me tomorrow, same time." Emily told him only he could perform this activity, and that he was chosen by a special council for this task. He would honor the world by his actions. She advised him not to let anyone else, except his wife, know about the subject of the phone call.

Carlos patted Spooky, and sat at the small, wood table to eat. "You sounded uneasy, my love." Darsella finished putting food on the table and took her seat opposite Carlos. "Talk to me."

"I am asked by this woman, Emily, to find a precious gem they call a Wisdom Stone." Carlos ate a little pasta. "I am chosen, she said, to find this gem. I am to meet them at Chichen Itza. This mission may take two or three days to complete." He put down his fork and caught her gaze. He explained the importance of the Mission to humankind and its timeliness. "What do you think?"

Darsella smiled. "Maybe you are chosen to complete a great mission, I think you are honored by these people as a part of it. You should go."

"Thank you, beloved." Carlos drank some coffee. "You help me choose to go or not. I will take some leave from work and venture on to this important mission."

25

MUNICH

The air felt cold to Halmar Fitzburg, and a quiet, numbing chill filled the room. Four men at one end of the long, wooden table discussed their next moves. Halmar wore a desperate countenance and tapped his long fingernails into the wood.

"I have three men in prison in Russia and three more in jail at Sedona in the United States. There are only four of us left to plan our next moves. You three cannot be everywhere at once. I must travel to Russia to bargain for the three there. What do you suggest?"

Kent leaned forward. "We have stopped their mission to bring those stones into the world, so the only thing they can do is teach."

Franko interrupted. "Maybe we have stopped them. But that Greg guy is determined. If he can find a way to work around the missing stone, he will. So I say we still need to watch them."

"Yes, I see your point." Kent said. "But the teaching has got to stop. Right now that is the only thing we can take action against."

Friedrick leaned back in his chair. "I agree with both of you. We need to keep watching them. But right now we need to take action.

Why not kidnap that Shannon woman in Madrid? It would have worked for Monsignor Terkenni if those two snoopers minded their own business. He was almost there when that Isabel woman busted into the place where he held his prisoner."

"We could get into trouble for pulling something like that." Fitzburg raised his brow. "But I have an idea. We could keep her hostage in her house. That way we do not cross borders and we could threaten to take her somewhere."

The three men nodded. "We should do it," said Kent.

"Okay, the three of you put your heads together and come up with a plan." The general stood. "I have to line up travel to Russia. Meet me here in the morning and we will firm up our next steps." He opened the door and left.

Kent moved closer to the other two. "We need to draw that Greg guy to Madrid, when we hold the woman. I still have a score to settle. So here is what I have in mind."

26

CHICHEN ITZA

fter arriving in Cancun two hours earlier, Greg savored the
warm sun, the perfect water temperature, and the warm, soft
sand under his feet. He glanced at Isabel sitting across from
him. "So you have the routine down relating to our Recipient?"

"Yeah, pretty much." Isabel caught his gaze, and then stared
out over the ocean. "I think it more important that I get the Stone
search details down pat."

Greg nodded. "I agree. But it will come as we move through it."

Carlos arrived at the Cancun airport on the afternoon flight
from Honduras. His dark eyes shifted beneath heavy black eye-
brows, while he talked with them and awaited his baggage.
His dark skin and stocky build reminded Greg of some Native
Americans he had visited in Sedona. Isabel and Greg accompanied
Carlos to his room.

"I am so glad you are willing to come here so quickly." Greg
smiled. "This Mission has a timeline and we need to complete our
work as soon as we can."

Carlos smiled. "I am most honored to serve. We can finish this mission fast, for you two know what to do and I know the land. We make a good team."

Greg gave Carlos more detailed information than Emily was able to do over the phone. When they met for their evening meal, they completed the details for the next day.

Isabel, Greg and Carlos pulled into the parking lot at Chichen Itza just as the sun reached its zenith. They gathered their gear and hiked toward the Temple of the Warriors and the accompanying Group of a Thousand Columns. Those two areas contained hundreds of columns and many large and small buildings, which Carlos felt would make excellent hiding places for the Stone. Greg was glad that he had contacted a friend he had met in Hawaii to get archeological "passes" and permission to explore the areas not open to the public. He felt that the Activation would take place underground, and they would need access to the whole area.

As they strolled past the Temple of Kukulcan, Greg said, "I read that the pyramid temples built by the Mayans were constructed one on top of another, about every 50 years or so, relating to a 'cycle of time.' Their pyramids were built geometrically and expressed correlation with time and cycles. The Temple of Kukulcan had four sides and nine harmonious platforms, each with 91 steps, giving a sum of 364. Adding the final step onto the platform at the top, totaled 365 for a one-year cycle. It always amazes me how particular the ancients were in using the stars and other celestial bodies to set time and conduct ceremonies."

"Well said, my American friend." said Carlos.

Isabel joined the conversation. "I too read in a book Shannon loaned me that the Mayans, like the Atlantian and other spiritual peoples, have intuitive knowledge of things modern 'man' only dreams of. With all its technology and scientific knowledge, the Western world has yet to delve into the mystical mind that outperforms it all. Yet peoples like the Mayans and Incas, created cities and lived a life centered in the knowledge of their own greatness as Divine Beings."

They each took a section for the search even though Greg or Isabel would have to find Carlos should they locate the where-abouts of the Stone. But since searching for a hidden Stone among all of those columns seemed a lengthy exercise, they'd save valuable time. Greg chose the Temple of the Warriors so he could go higher to spot other possible areas, and to watch for suspicious characters. The other two explored the many columns surrounding the tem-ple; Isabel near the temple and Carlos east of it.

Once he reached the top of the temple, Greg noticed other col-umns, probably supporting a roof hundreds of years ago. From his lofty site Greg also surveyed the whole complex for their opponents lurking about, if by some chance they learned of his whereabouts. Much of Chichen Itza had been restored, and so a lot of what he observed hadn't been there when Carlos's Stone was hidden. All the more reason to search underground, he surmised. They had planned to meet in front of the temple after two hours, or in the event someone found the Stone. So finding nothing of importance, he made his way down the temple steps to meet the other two, and found Isabel and Carlos in deep discussion.

"I hope you had better luck than me," he said approaching them.

"Ah, Greg. We were jus' wondering where you hide from us. Isabel say you probably nap somewhere and enjoy the sun," Carlos said with a chuckle.

Greg smiled. "I might as well have been, for all I've found."

"Like you, we find nothing." Carlos said with a frown. "I think I make a quick choice that take us behind the temple and columns."

Isabel smiled. "Carlos has another place he thinks is a better choice; the steam bath."

"Yes, I remember reading about it," said Greg. "It seems to have many nooks and crannies, so to speak, where a Stone could be hidden. Let's go there."

They hiked down the paved area until they reached the steam baths. These baths were a series of buildings above "shower stalls" built so that water above them gave people a shower. The buildings seemed to be for baths and for changing clothes. After peeking in several "nooks", Greg sat on a piece of concrete.

"We need to spread out again," Greg said, "and search. These baths are small, but lead to some complex places we could search. Let's meet back here in an hour."

Once again, they each took an area to search. Greg felt that if the adept wanted to hide the Stone 400 years ago, it would have to stay hidden regardless of what destruction or eventual reconstruction took place. He found a small cranny in the back that looked like it had held up over the years. He searched for anything that might be movable.

"This looks interesting." He knelt and ran his finger over the edge of some stones that seemed a little different from the rest. Since his hour was up, he met the others and told them what he had found.

Isabel put her hands on her hips. "It is good that you found something because I found nothing, nor did Carlos. Let's go."

After arriving at the cranny Greg showed them the odd looking stones.

Carlos stood near it and then turned. "I feel this is right place."

Greg and Isabel knelt and used their small picks to see if the stones were removable.

"Here, this feels loose." Isabel pulled at the edge of a stone, and then the corner just popped out and turned. She pulled it loose and the stone next to it also came free. Underneath where they had been was a crevice. "What do you make of it.?"

Greg examined the crevice. He reached down towards the wall next to it. "I feel a…" Unexpectedly the wall moved. Greg jumped back. "I must have hit a latch of some kind." He pulled on the piece of wall and it opened about half a meter. He shone his light inside. "We may have found our entrance."

Greg moved inside and spotted a downward path that seemed to go under the bath house building. Isabel and Carlos came inside and moved down the path. Greg closed the wall by pulling on a piece of wood on the inside of the wall. Isabel flashed her light around the cave-like path. She spied wooden beams above held there by wood struts.

"It looks like someone dug this and made a tunnel." Isabel said.

Greg followed the other two for about ten meters. The tunnel appeared to be about a meter wide and two meters high. "Yes, and they did great job of it too."

Then Carlos stopped. "I feel heat. My hands feel warm. I think we are close to Stone." Then the tunnel ended.

Greg pointed to a cleft. "Looks like an opening over there." They found an alcove with a line of large pegs. Isabel checked for something loose. They wiggled and pulled the pegs and some rock ledges, but nothing happened.

"What have we here?" Carlos found a dark place below them with a cranny. He kicked at it. Suddenly, his foot went through the earth into a hole up to his knee. "Agh…a hole." He pulled his leg out, then sent a beam of light inside. There was another large peg about half way down. He pulled on it, and it came out easily.

At this point, a soft feeling of energy emanated from within the hole left by the peg. Carlos got busy with the task of removing some dirt and found a black box. Isabel and Greg peered over Carlos's shoulders holding their lights, while he removed the black box.

"Ah, what is inside?"

When he opened the box, a soft glow emerged from a pouch. Carlos picked it up, and held it close to his heart, and said, "I have the Stone."

He opened the pouch, and a pink light filled the dark area drowning out Greg and Isabel's lights. Carlos then closed the pouch and put it in his fanny pack, turned and said. "We are done."

They quietly made their way through the tunnel, ascended the ramp, and then checked for other visitors, before opening the wall. They all stepped out of the cranny into the fresh air and sunlight.

The sunlight, however, neared the horizon, and they made their way to the car while the last light vanished from the clouds above. Isabel drove and Carlos sat in the back with his Pink Stone.

Greg had checked for mail on his way to their room, but again nothing was there. *Hope Emily and Karl are okay. I would hate to see Fitzburg's men show up here.* After a shower and change of clothes, he joined the other two for a great dinner. Carlos shared his experience with the Stone after returning to his room.

"I gazed at her pink color; it is beautiful, no? And then I look at gold line down her middle. She speak to me as I caress her. I feel like I connect to her when I open box. When I put box next to me on side of tub when washing, she spoke to me. She give me so many ideas and information, I feel like I know her personality."

"Exactly as it should, Carlos." Greg smiled. "The better you and the Stone connect, the easier it will be for us to find and Activate it, er her."

Carlos continued his tale. "I see a swirling rainbow vortex that pulled me into a golden-white light. There I saw a figure, like angel hover above me. The figure spoke, and tell me about the Stone's history. The female figure named Charlon, told me personal stories about her relations with the Stone. Charlon tell me to 'seek the pool'. It will lead me to the Activation site."

"That is what we need, Carlos, the location of the site." Greg smiled. "We need to find that place in the morning and be very careful. It has been my experience that the 'bad guys' show up when we are ready to go to the activation site."

27

MADRID

full moon shined brightly through the large window in Shannon's living room. Awed by its beauty, she stepped outside into the cool night air, sat on the porch swing, and lay back against its pillows. The week had gone well as another class graduated, and shared how much they had learned in that short amount of time. *If only Karl were here more often. But right now, he has his own classes to teach.*

Shannon continued to enjoy the moonlight and stars for awhile, until she heard the sound of her cell phone. "Maybe it's Karl." She hurried to answer the phone just inside the front door.

"Hi Karl, I hoped it was you. How are things in Sedona?" She moved back through the door and sat on the swing again.

Karl's voice came in clear. "We had a bit of a confrontation with Fitzburg's men, but Emily and Greg arrived in time to take care of it. At least for now. They are demanding the closing of our classrooms, which, of course, Emily refused. So, we'll see how it all pans out. Call me on the other phone when you get a chance." They chatted awhile longer, and then Shannon got up to go into the house to make the call Karl mentioned using the encrypted phone.

A man's voice came from behind her. "Good evening, Shannon."

She turned and found two tall men standing there. "What do you want?"

A third man came from the side of the porch. "We want to join you for the evening. Why don't you step inside so we can talk?"

"I don't know who you are or why you are here, but I am on my way to town, and don't have time right now." She turned, stepped onto the pavement and opened the car door.

One of the men put his hand on the door. "I am Kent, and think your trip can wait. What we have to tell you is much more important to you." He grabbed her shoulder. "Go inside."

She resisted for a moment, considering whether to use the limited amount of Kung Fu she had learned from Isabel. *He's too big and I am too inexperienced. Besides there are two other men.*

The three men surrounded her, and then Kent pulled her inside the house and shoved her onto the couch. "We have been waiting for the right moment so that we can pass on to you a message from our leader."

"And who is this leader of yours?" Shannon barked.

Kent smiled. "I thought you would figure it out by now. General Fitzburg, of course. He wanted us to tell you that we want all classes stopped immediately."

"I don't know what you are talking about." Shannon gave him a stern look.

Kent leaned forward. "We are talking about you simply closing your classroom."

Just then Shannon's cell phone sounded.

"Answer it, but you had better be careful about what you say." Kent handed the phone to her.

"Hello this is Shannon." The voice on the other end was Karl and asked about the phone call he had mentioned earlier. Unable to answer Karl, she said "Well I have been quite busy since then.

Perhaps another time. I need to go." She pushed the off button and put the phone beside her.

Kent took the phone. "Now let us continue."

She began to get apprehensive and sat back against the couch while tension gripped her whole body. "I cannot tell you that I will close this classroom. It is not my call. Emily is in charge. When she gives me the go ahead to close the classroom, I will do it."

"Really?" Kent slapped her face hard. "Well maybe you should call her and get permission. If not, we will just keep you here; then you will not be available to teach."

By this time, Shannon was shaking and holding the side of face that burned from the slap. "Okay, I will call her."

She dialed Emily's number. When Emily answered, Shannon explained the situation, almost in tears. "Let me talk to one of them," Emily said.

Shannon handed the phone to Kent who seemed to be in charge. "This is Kent. What do you have to say?"

"What I have to tell you is that we are not closing the classrooms." Emily's voice came through strong. "We told the men here earlier that we would not close them. They are now in jail."

Kent's face formed a scowl. "For that you will be sorry. We have no choice then, but to hold your friend hostage, maybe blow up the classroom, or kidnap some students until you satisfy our demands." He pushed the off button.

28

CHICHEN ITZA

*sabel, Carlos, and Greg arrived back at Chichen Itza mid-*morning, excited about new information from Carlos's Stone. His latest vision showed a red spot in the middle of a pool of water, and an underwater cave. The only bodies of water they knew of at Chichen Itza were the sacrificial well known as the Sacred Cenote, and another water-hole that the Mayans used as a water supply. They went to the Sacred Cenote first. Greg had gotten scuba gear, including wetsuits and waterproof lights, from a rental place in Cancun.

Even though they had cleared their intent to explore and possibly dig with authorities, and The Council had once again opened the doors for them, diving into a sacred well might draw attention. They would need to use caution and carefully approach their descent into the water. Greg had read that occasionally the water turns red due to the appearance of algae with red seeds. The red area Carlos had seen must signal the beginning, or end, of that growth.

When they arrived at the huge water-filled hole, its size and depth surprised Greg. "I had no idea it was this big. I read that its

179

use as a sacrificial pool was confirmed when a man had dredged and dived in it during the 1860's, and found skeletons amongst its artifacts. Spooky."

The three had hiked away from the observation point, and about a quarter way around, when Isabel spotted the red area that Carlos saw in his vision. They hurried to it, careful of the increasing brush and low hanging trees.

Stopping just above the red spot, they cleared a small area of thorny brush, and got scuba gear and climbing apparatus from their packs. Neither the three meter diameter red spot nor the area above it could be easily seen from the public observation point; keeping their activities unobserved. They had each brought one tiny air supply tank in their packs, and hoped it would be enough.

Greg drove a spike into the rocky edge, attached a rope, tied it to his waist, and let himself down into the murky water. He sensed negative energy and figured it must be due to the sacrificed corpses lying there all those years. He could not easily see through the water, especially in the red part, but further down it cleared some. He descended near the middle of the red spot, and figured he could explore from that point out on both sides. Greg could see the stone wall even through the murk, and he thought that a hole of some kind should stand out. When his foot touched what he assumed to be the bottom, he swam along the wall. The goggles he wore kept his eyes from becoming irritated and increased the depth of his view. He zigzagged up and down, while swimming away from the rope and hoped to cover the maximum amount of wall in a minimum of time.

After he'd explored maybe seven meters out from where he had started, he turned and came back using opposite zigs and zags. He passed where he started and swam through the same pattern on the opposite side. He finished his search pattern, finding no hole or clue to one. He surfaced, lifted his mask, and yelled.

"I cannot find an entrance. I have been all over the place." He took a deep breath.

They simultaneously yelled, "Go deeper." They turned toward each other and laughed.

"Okay, I got it." Greg shouted. "Throw me a shovel."

They lowered it to the water's edge.

He grabbed the folded shovel and let go of the rope. His feet had touched what seemed to be the bottom on his first dive, but it hadn't occurred to him that debris from trees, grass, storms and millions of tourists had accumulated for many years. But first, he had to locate where to start digging. He figured that the cave entrance he sought would leave some kind of telltale reference to its location, like a hole or shallow depression at the bottom of the large pool. Circling the Cenote, Greg finally pinpointed one area opposite the red spot that displayed a dip or sort of channel towards the wall. He'd start there.

He placed his feet on the bottom, and then plunged the shovel into the soft ground. When he pulled the debris up with the shovel, his whole body went with it. He floated back to the surface, and realized he needed weights while digging. He surfaced again. "I need weights. What have you got up there?" They found some heavy rocks, tied them to a rope, and lowered them to Greg. He tied them around his waist and returned to digging. He dug slowly to keep the bits of debris from leaving his shovel and clouding the water. He dumped it behind him as far as possible.

When Greg had removed about two feet of leaves, branches and other debris, his shovel sank into the wall slightly. He moved it around, and it went in further. He dug deeper, wanting to go faster, but restrained himself to keep from clouding the water. Each shovel-full revealed a larger portion of the hole. He dug for another twenty minutes, enlarging the hole to about half a meter. Greg found it plenty big enough for him to safely enter, and the water got cleaner the further he swam. The rope became taut and Greg knew he had to go back and prepare for finding a cave. He swam back to the Cenote, and pulled himself to the surface.

"I found a tunnel. We need to make preparations to explore."

The other two pulled him up. Isabel and Carlos donned their wetsuits, put their "exploring" gear into a waterproof pack, and

left the rest in the brush. They rigged three ropes; one tied around
Greg's waist, one around Carlos's waist, and one tied to a nearby
tree that they would use as a "travel" line once they found a cave.
Isabel would stay behind until the other two substantiated the tunnel led to the cave they wanted. She would stay on top until they
were ready.

Carlos and Greg got into the water and swam through the hole
Greg had uncovered. They kept close to the top of the rounded,
sometimes jagged and irregular underwater cave, searching for a
place to surface. After about 20 meters they found a place where
the solid rock tunnel gave way to open water, and surfaced.
Flashing their lights about, they saw two cave entrances — one
on either side.

Greg pulled himself up to one side, and then helped Carlos.
They stood, and scanned the walls and ceilings of both caves with
their lights. Greg tied a safety rope to a protrusion at the mouth of
one cave.

"This must be what we are looking for," said Greg. "Why don't
you see if you can determine which cave we should seek, while I go
get Isabel?"

"Maybe I get guidance," Carlos said, and sat against the wall,
his eyes closed.

Greg swam back to the Cenote and its surface. "We are ready.
Lower yourself down here." She joined him and they made their
way to the cave.

Once Isabel and Greg got into the cave they removed their
wetsuits.

Carlos got up and removed his wet suit. "We go this way." He
strode into the cave and they followed. After about 30 meters, they
crossed a second water tunnel and trudged upward. The walls
changed dramatically, giving way to smooth, almost shiny tex-
tures. They encountered many turns and then the cave split. One
path had petroglyphs of people, animals and the sun. Drawings of
people climbing the steps of a pyramid and carrying what appeared
to be gold. They decided to follow the petroglyphs, since the other

tunnel had none. The passage finally widened into a room similar to the one they had discovered at Machu Picchu.

The room looked like a burial chamber for royalty, adorned with paintings, altars and many artifacts and jewels. Greg marveled at the complexity and beauty of the jewelry and other artifacts, while Isabel held some of the jewelry above her examining its extravagance. They all felt the energy of the room, and Carlos knew that it was the ceremonial site for the Stone.

Carlos removed his Pink Stone from the leather pouch and sat with it cupped in his hands. He closed his eyes, getting instructions for the ceremony. After a few minutes he arose, and set the Stone at the center of a small, rounded pedestal. Immediately, it glowed and grew brighter each second until it illumined the whole room. A Being cloaked by bright light emerged above the Stone, radiating a similar light, filled with pink and specks of violet.

"Greetings friends. I am Charlon," the being said. "I honor you and your selflessness in honoring Mother Earth and the peoples that inhabit her. There are not many in your world who would endure the hardships and danger you have encountered. Each Activation is a gift to your fellow humans and blesses them."

"My dear Carlos, take the water you have collected and pour it over the Pink Stone and the altar upon which it rests."

Carlos removed a vial and poured its contents as Charlon had directed.

Isabel and Greg gave each other blank looks wondering where he got the water.

Carlos backed away from the altar. A Golden-Pink ray of light came from above and lit the altar and its contents.

Charlon's image grew larger and brighter while she spoke the Activation Message.

"This Stone calls the Golden-Pink Ray, representing Compassion. What more can one Being feel for another than Unconditional Love? And Compassion is Unconditional Love in action. All the Great Masters taught us to reach for Love and that embracing Love was the root of human existence. Some looked at a world of suffering and put

Compassion above all else. It is the motivating force creating ways to relieve suffering. Within the compelling need to stop the suffering is the foundation of Unconditional Love. Mother Teresa was the shining light of Compassion. She moved through the streets of Calcutta attending to those in need."

A silver-white light appeared and grew brighter, and within it an image of Mother Teresa emerged. She smiled and bowed to them. Charlon continued.

"How much easier does compassion aid each human to attend to the needs of her neighbor, his brother, or her sister? Can anyone ignore their cry for help? What is suffering? Is it not separation from God? Is it not separation from each other? You are all one human family living together upon a planet that supports your Oneness. Yet humanity embraces separation. Most find 'different' offensive, and separate themselves from all that is unlike themselves. Can these beings not see the suffering caused by that way of thinking?

Compassion is remembering that you are all One. Everything on your planet, including your planet, is in Oneness with you. Remember. Awaken. Stop the suffering. Use Compassion to return to Oneness. This Golden-Pink Ray will aid each human in bringing Compassion into his or her life. Look at the world around you — your immediate world. Compassionately tend to it. A smile. A tender touch. A gift. A favor. All of these and more speak of Compassion. Oh humanity, you have felt separate for so long. Love one another. Be Compassionate with your Planet. She is suffering, and needs your help. Love her as She Loves you".

Charlon stopped speaking and silence prevailed, until a vibration building within the Stone and radiating from the altar outward, caused all that was in the room to shake. The three occupants fell backward and slumped against the wall. The vibrations formed into waves of light moving outward from the Stone's center toward all parts of the planet. The vibration then steadied and Charlon spoke for the last time.

"It is finished. Go and spread compassion throughout your world. We bless your efforts and go with you."

She stood by the Stone and above the altar. A canopy enclosed the Stone and formed a shield around it, leaving Charlon standing behind it like a glowing candle. "One more thing, Greg." Her voice came to him in his mind. "Your final Sacred Site is Easter Island. Blessings."

Greg thanked her. *So that is how Emily got those messages.* He considered how compassion worked in his life. Had he felt compassion for the "crooks" that were trying to stop them? Did they deserve compassion? *All beings deserve compassion.* That thought came through so powerfully he almost fell to the rocky floor. *I guess I need to reconsider my position on compassion.* He recovered from the jolt and joined the others.

When they left the room and entered the tunnel, they heard a rumbling sound. Looking back they watched the room's entrance disappear. Greg felt relieved that no one could find it easily and noticed the other two with surprised looks. Had he not witnessed similar miracles, he too would have shared their wonder.

"I am so touched," Carlos said. "During the ceremony, all my mistakes came to me in my mind like sticks in a rushing river. I pick the 'sticks' out of the river and throw them in the center of Light. And then I feel peace."

Isabel smiled. "I had a similar experience with 'potholes' in my 'road of life.' And I used the Light to fill them."

They made their way to the water's edge, where they all donned their wetsuits in silence and untied the safety rope. They got back into the cold water, and swam to the Cenote. They pulled on the rope tied to the tree above and found it loose. They looked at each other quizzically. Greg pulled on the ropes tied around their waists and they were loose.

Greg searched the wall with his light, and found no sign of the ropes. Isabel and Carlos also searched for the ropes, with equal lack of success. So Greg dove back in the water, swam in the direction the ropes had been, and followed the wall up to the surface — nothing. They all lay in the water like dead snakes.

Greg had the collapsible hook used at Mt. Shasta, and had Isabel pull it from his pack while he tread water, and tied it to a rope. Then, while Isabel and Carlos pointed their lights at the top of the Cenote, Greg made several attempts at catching something with the hook. Having to tread water while throwing the wet rope in almost total darkness, proved overwhelming. Greg asked Carlos to hold his waist while Isabel aimed her light on some bushes. But after a dozen more tries at several places, he quit.

Carlos asked to try, and Greg gave the hook to him. After his sixth attempt he hooked a bush further away from the edge. He pulled himself up, but when he got halfway to the top the hook slipped off the bush. His body fell backwards into the water with a loud splash, and Greg and Isabel had to duck out of the way when the hook followed. They were exhausted, cold, wet, and defeated. They decided to go back into the tunnel where it was at least dry.

They swam back to the cave area, followed the tunnel toward the Activation site, and then took the other branch. It sloped upward, and turned several times until opening into a large, round room. It had what Isabel described as tables and chairs made of stone and wood, and many pieces of pottery. It may have been a community center of some kind. They removed their wet suits and gear, and put them in a corner.

"What you think happen to ropes, amigo?" Carlos asked.

"Someone must have untied them, because I could find no trace of them being cut." Greg said. "It could have been a park attendant wondering what it was doing there, or . . ." His voice trailed off, and he sat silently considering the possibilities.

"Could someone have been watching us," said Isabel, "and took the rope to keep us from returning? If so, we might be in bigger trouble than just having to spend the night in a cold hole in the ground."

Carlos smiled. "We come out okay tomorrow. If bad guys did show up then they be gone when we awake."

All they had in their waterproof pack were some lightweight emergency blankets. They had nothing to produce warmth, except their lights. They had not expected to stay below more than a few hours, and had only packed bare necessities. Each of them wrapped themselves in a blanket and huddled together.

Greg awoke, startled by a sound from above and wondered if it were daylight. The other two awakened soon thereafter. They gathered their gear and headed back to the water-cave. They repeated their activities of yesterday, and were soon on the surface of the water. Dawn bloomed with rays of sunlight catching clouds above Chichen Itza. Greg swam around the Cenote hunting for an area to throw his hook. He found a spot not far from their place of descent, and had Carlos hold his waist while he tossed the hook upward. It caught the branch of a small tree, and he checked its security. He pulled himself up and tied the rope around the trunk. He then helped the others, scrutinizing the area for anyone who might see them. But they were probably too early for any tourists and Greg felt relieved.

Greg unhooked the rope, and they made their way back to where they started yesterday. When they got there, they discovered that everything was gone — no spike, no packs, nothing. They searched the area in case they had lost their bearings, but found nothing. After reaching the pathway to the Cenote, they found their way to the parking lot.

They then made their way to one of the hotels and asked for someone connected with the site. The clerk called, and in a few minutes they were talking to the night watchman. But he knew nothing about equipment or backpacks. They would have to wait until the lost and found opened to check about their bags.

They drove back to their hotel, changed and had breakfast. While they ate, Greg's phone sounded. "Hello, my dear Emily. What news have you? What? We will go there immediately." He clicked the off button and turned to Isabel.

"We have to leave as soon as possible. Kent and two other men are holding Shannon hostage so that we will give in and close our classrooms."

Isabel frowned. "They will pay for this I promise."

29

MADRID, SPAIN

The Madrid airport provided an easy exit to the rental car area for Isabel and Greg to quickly find their car. The drive to Shannon's house took about 30 minutes. They parked down the street so as not to alert anyone, should the renegades be outside and see a rental car parked near her home.

They crept to the side of the house and listened through a window. They heard a strange male voice speaking. "You understand why we are here, don't you?" No answer came forth from Shannon. "Only to persuade young Emily to close those cursed classrooms. Nothing more, nothing less." Silence followed.

Greg couldn't be sure how many men were inside, but there were at least two. "Isn't there a small basement access somewhere?" Isabel nodded. He scanned the areas of the house at ground level. She moved around the perimeter on her knees to avoid detection.

"Over here." She pointed to a spot at the far-corner of the bungalow.

Greg scooted to the corner. He pulled on the handle of a wooden door. It didn't move. "Damn, it's locked."

"Anything locked can be unlocked with the right tools." Isabel examined the door. She reached into her coat pocket and pulled out a kit containing various tools for cracking locks. "I brought this 'just in case'." After pushing a long rod-shaped tool in, she used two others to quickly unlock the door. "Done." She opened the door and disappeared. Greg followed quietly.

Only the outside light gave them a view of what was ahead. Isabel pulled a tiny LED flashlight from her pocket. "Over there are stairs." She quietly climbed them, and then stopped at the top listening for conversations. She came back down the stairs to where Greg stood. "It sounds like they are in the kitchen, or near it. They should not be able to see that door from where they are. What do you think?"

Greg glanced at the door. "It sounds risky. Once they see us, the element of surprise disappears, and it is just us against them. They probably have weapons."

Isabel nodded. "I agree, plus they may have Shannon in a position where they could threaten her to ward off attackers. So what do we do?"

"Surprise is our best option I think." Greg stared at the ceiling. "We wait until it gets dark."

Tired from their trip from Mexico, they laid on a spare mattress. They agreed to take turns sleeping. Three hours later, darkness came. Isabel and Greg practiced moving in darkness, *sensing* where things were instead of seeing where they were. This is how martial artists kept from being surprised by an enemy. Once they felt ready, they climbed the stairs. Isabel tried the door and quietly opened it to darkness. A noise and faint light coming from the direction of the living room told them the TV was playing.

They got down in a scouting position, low to the floor and ready for attack or defense, as they moved closer to the sounds. Greg rose a bit so that he could peek over the chair right in front of him at the far end of the living room. He could see the TV and three people watching it. Shannon sat in a chair with her arms behind her, evidently tied together. Two men sat on the couch adjacent to the chair. He could not see if either had weapons.

Greg kneeled down beside Isabel. He pointed toward the couch and indicated that they crawl in that direction. She nodded. Ready to encounter the men, they quietly made their way to the sofa's edge, and then dove toward the men's feet. They pulled the surprised men to the floor, twisted their arms behind them, and tied them to their feet with the rope they brought from the basement.

"What . . . what's happening? Who are you?" Kent yelled, evidently awakening from sleep on a nearby chair that had been out of their view earlier.

The other men only grunted and cursed, while wiggling, trying to break loose of their bounds.

"Isabel, Greg! Thank God." Shannon screamed and managed a slight smile.

Kent leaped at Greg, pulling him to the floor. "You again. This time I will finish you." He grabbed Greg's ankles and swung him around knocking down Isabel. The big man's height and strength gave him a momentary advantage. He let go of Greg's legs just as he approached the front window. Greg's body crashed through the window and landed on the front porch. Kent began untying his comrade's ropes, when Isabel grabbed his legs and pushed him to the floor. She then kicked his head and stomped a stiletto heel into his stomach. Kent groaned and tried to get up.

By this time, Greg had recovered and ran back into the room. Just as one of the men attempted to get up, he kicked the man's chest and then his head; knocking him out. Isabel kept a foot on Kent's throat, while Greg untied Shannon. Shannon immediately grabbed a nearby wooden lamp and brought the bottom of it across Kent's head like a baseball bat knocking him unconscious. The three of them then managed to tie Kent and the other two back to back in a circle.

"Where did you come from? Friedrick asked. "How did you know we were here?"

Greg glared at him. "We got word that you might hold Shannon hostage, to seal your demands of our closing the classrooms. Good thing."

They called the police, and charged the men with holding Shannon hostage and kidnapping. It was a struggle keeping Kent bound and moving him to the police vehicle even thought he was still groggy from the blow. But finally, with their help, Kent was contained.

After the three men and police left, they all sat and rested for awhile discussing The Cause's second attempt at closing the classes down. Then Isabel made tea, and they all had something to eat.

"I can't do this anymore." Shannon's whole body shook as she ate. "I will end my lease on this house and move to Sedona with Karl. I feel like a sitting duck here after all that has happened this past year." She nervously sipped her tea. "This classroom will have to go. At least it will satisfy The Cause that we gave in to this one, anyway."

Isabel put her hand on Shannon's arm. "I understand and am totally with you. Meanwhile, I would like you to join me. Greg will explain."

"I am ready to offer you a vacation, of sorts." Greg gave her a half-smile. "In order to keep Fitzburg guessing, I need to return to Sedona with Emily. Meanwhile, we have one more Activation to finish. We would like you and Isabel to complete the last Wisdom Stone search and Activation on Easter Island. The two of you will leave in a day or so and travel to Chili. From there you will fly to Easter Island. How does that sound?"

Shannon smiled. "A chance to be part of the last Stone search and Activation sounds great. I have missed those days we spent two years ago. I will be ready."

"Great. Get your things together and be prepared to travel in two days. We only have six more days to meet our deadline of 11-11-2011." Greg touched her shoulder. "Meanwhile, Emily will contact the last Recipient and arrange your flights. We will contact you with a somewhat cryptic call tomorrow and let you know it is time to move."

30

PULTRE, CHILE

The Andean sky continuously changed as Shaman Kania Ke hiked up the craggy trail. He turned and swept his eyes across the vast expanse and the town of Pultre, where the Mayan lived most of the time. He reflected on his arrival to this communal town four years earlier. After living in the highlands of Mexico most of his life, he had ventured to Peru, where he explored the mountains around Machu Picchu. It was there that he felt a calling to Chile. His arrival was hailed as the fulfillment of an ancient prophecy; a wise Mayan would bring them together and heal long-held wounds of shame and guilt. The Shaman felt honored by his notoriety even if it was only for a small group.

The Shaman cave was still six kilometers away and Kania wondered about the graying sky. He would spend the night at the cave performing a sacred ritual to open his mind to the Spirit World. Kania Ke never missed a full moon ceremony, and this one seemed very important; something was about to change, and he needed to tune in to its character.

As he hiked up the faint trail, he thought about the events he had experienced lately. The 93 years he had lived upon this planet had not given him the closeness and love he felt at the Mayan celebration of ancestors two weeks ago. Both close friends and strangers displayed to him a camaraderie he had never experienced. The talk of the celebration focused on Mayan Prophecies and the expectations of outcomes in 2012. This year would be a year of transformation and a return to their Mayan heritage.

An hour later Kania Ke stopped for a rest. He drank some water and ate a papaya and some cacao nibs. While he ate, he took in the scenery below. In the distance, the Pacific Ocean mirrored the late afternoon sunlight. *It is good. My heart is filled to overflowing. May God reflect onto me, what the ocean and rocks tell me.* A condor flew overhead, and then disappeared in the direction of the cave. *A sign that I am blessed on this journey.*

He finished his repast and journeyed onward. An hour later, he arrived at his destination. The Shaman Cave sat along the side of a mountain peak. To reach it, he had to climb a series of cliffs that prevented most people from entering the site. The cave's Guardians stood watch at its entrance as well. These Ancestral Beings kept the space sacred by setting up an etheric field of energy around it. The Shaman felt this energy the closer he got to the cave.

After 30 more minutes of climbing, he approached the cave. Kania Ke stood outside of the entrance and asked permission to enter. He then sat and bowed, thanking his Ancestors for permission to use this sacred place. He performed a blessing, gathered his belongings, and strode into the depths. An immediate feeling of peace washed over him, and a sense of belonging and brotherhood.

Kania Ke prepared for the Full Moon Ceremony at the cave's mouth. He spread several herbs in a circle, and then lit a cup filled with white sage that he placed in the center. He made an outer circle with stones from the cave and special gems he pulled from his bag. He finally spread corn like spokes, in four directions from the center.

With the ceremonial circle completed, Kania Ke prepared his evening meal. The Condor returned and circled above the wheel he had built. The Shaman folded his hands and put them to his chest with a bow to the Condor. The bird then landed near the top of the cave as if ready to join the ceremony. Kania Ke built a fire off to one side of a ledge away from the sacred circle, and heated the ingredients for the tortillas. He put herbs, beans, peppers, and tomato into each tortilla and enjoyed his dinner, watching the setting sun sink below the ocean. As darkness arrived, Kania Ke finished his meal and then prepared himself for the ceremony.

He donned his ceremonial clothing, black leather pants and a white leather vest. Strings of various kinds of beads hung around his neck and he wore beaded bracelets on his wrists. The Shaman covered his face and bare arms with black and white paint, then drew a red circle on his forehead. When the moon appeared overhead, the Shaman lit the sage and began his ancient dance around the circle.

After 30 minutes, Kania Ke sat in the center of the circle, moving the burnt sage container to the side. He then stared at the moon, recited sacred mantras, and chanted for an hour. Then all grew quiet while the Shaman sat in silence. Two hours later, Kania Ke got up, noticed the Condor had left, bowed, and then returned to the cave where he prepared his bed for the night. He fell asleep quickly, already in a dreamlike state.

The next morning, the Mayan Shaman dismantled the circle and returned the cave to the way it was when he arrived. He gathered his belongings, and headed back down the mountain. He spoke to Spirit. "Oh great mystery you have once again blessed me with your sacred fire. Thank you for this blessed journey. Mother moon has acknowledged me as well and I thank her for her radiance and peace. I am your servant always and walk in the wisdom of your Love. I am blessed."

Later in the afternoon, the Shaman entered his bungalow at the edge of Pultre. His black cat, Leon, greeted him at the door. "Ah your master had such a time, my friend, the Gods look upon us with many blessings." He changed this clothes, ate a snack, and was about to nap when he noticed a blinking light. "What is this, we had a call?" He listened to the recorded message.

"Kania Ke, my name is Emily and I have a request for your services to assist our world." She gave him a number to call, after a brief description of the Mission's task. "We also have a deadline to meet. The Stone must be Activated on 11-11-2011 at sunset. That only gives us six days." The Shaman called the number given and after a brief conversation, agreed to meet Shannon and Isabel in Santiago in two days.

"I am famous Leon." The man patted the cat. "The world needs my services."

31

SEDONA, ARIZONA

The day after the phone call from Greg, Karl received an *encrypted* call from Shannon. "Hi Karl. I am excited about going to Chile and beyond, but I am finished here. When I complete my trip and the Mission is over, I intend to end my lease and move to Sedona. I can't take the constant barrage of attacks on my classroom, and now my house. This will also give you a chance to close a classroom and may keep Fitzburg at bay for awhile. What do you think?"

Karl smiled. "I think it is a great idea, not only because we will be together, but it will likely deter the similar attacks here and give us a chance to breathe. I can't wait." They chatted a little, and then Karl clicked the off button. He had to meet with Emily and Greg in an hour, but first, pick up Greg from the airport.

Later, in one room of Greg's adobe house rigged to protect them from outside listeners, the three tired heroes sat across from one another. Karl repeated his conversation with Shannon and how happy he was with her decision.

"I think she is on the right track," said Emily. "We can close classrooms they know about and continue running the others. While The Cause will still seek to impost their demands and watch us, I believe that over time they will see what they want – the classrooms closed. Besides, our main task is the Mission. It is there we must focus our efforts."

Greg drank some Chai tea. "I feel relieved that we may not have to continue defending classrooms, but at the same time, am concerned about the last Activation. So far, we have not detected movement on their part, but Shannon and Isabel need to fly out tomorrow unnoticed. Granted The Cause might think they are heading here, but they may also follow them if they suspect something is up."

"From what I have experienced with that gang of hoodlums," said Karl, "we always need to be ready for the unexpected and any possibility. They can be unsure of themselves despite how they act."

Greg leaned back. "I agree. We have kept them at bay so far, despite the power they wield and weapons they use. If I believed in luck, I would venture that so far we have been lucky. But what I know about how we have overcome their attacks is that we are perhaps, smarter than they are, and have out maneuvered them in each situation. While they attack thinking weapons, numbers, and size are more powerful than mental strategy, we have proven them wrong; so far at least."

"We will just have to know that the two of them will get to their rendezvous with Kania Ke safely and unnoticed." Emily smiled. "After all, we are being supported by the Universe. What greater 'ally' can we have?"

Karl slapped his open hand on the coffee table. "A safe and successful trip it is."

The other two put their hand on Karl's. "One Force, One Mind. Together we win."

32

CHILE, EASTER ISLAND

The Chilean sky turned blue below the clouds as the big plane made its landing at Santiago airport. Shannon and Isabel waited in the lobby for the Shaman, not knowing what he looked like. Soon, a small man with long, black hair, a black hat, and a tan, leather cape appeared. He strode towards them, stopped and bowed. "I am Kania Ke, at your service."

The two women stared at each other. "How did you know …?" Shannon blushed.

"I am shaman. Knowing is my calling." He bowed again.

The three moved through the gate for Easter Island, and then stopped at a café, since the flight wouldn't be leaving for another hour or so. "Your English is good. I am surprised," said Isabel.

"Ah, yes. I am schooled in English since I join many groups seeking experiences among the Andes; sort of a tour guide." He smiled.

They talked for awhile, getting to know each other, before leaving for their plane. After they boarded, they discussed areas of Easter Island, or Rapa Nui, to explore. Since they only had three days, their accuracy grew more important by the hour. Kania Ke had visited the island several times leading tours, and knew the landscape well. Upon landing near the town of Hanga Roa, they made their way to their hotel.

After a quick meal, they gathered their equipment, checked with the "land management" people and confirmed that they had permission to dig in the areas they had selected. Getting a green light, they rented a jeep, and took off towards the highest point on the island, Rano Aroi Volcano. There had been much discussion and exploration with maps, both before they left the States, and with Karl, Emily, and Greg's input, about where the most likely place the ancient Adepts would hide the last Wisdom Stone.

When they arrived at Rano Aroi, they found a shallow crater that looked to be no more than 20 feet deep.

"What do you make of it?" Isabel asked.

"Well, 400 years ago, when the Wisdom Stone was buried, this area looked quite different I am sure. In fact, there may have been few trees, since most of them were removed years before." Shannon said. "But compared to the geological age of this island, it seems not so long. We have always had to go by our intuition and signs we have found along the way. What do you think, Kania Ke?"

The Mayan Shaman climbed down the crater. "Yes, signs point the way to what you seek in life. That is how we find our path." He stooped at the bottom and ran his fingers across the grassy ground.

"Yes, of course." Shannon ran down the slope and joined the Shaman. Isabel stayed on top and explored the areas around the crater's circular path.

Two hours later, after exploring every foot of the crater and a perimeter 100 feet out from it, they came together in a grove of trees and sat. Shannon swept her arm in an arc. "It would seem that we may have come to the wrong conclusion about this location."

The Shaman folded his arms across his chest. "Would not help if in wrong place. We sit in trance."

Remembering how many of the Stones and Activation sites were found by meditation, Shannon said, "Good idea."

The Shaman led them in the meditation, sitting in a circle each touching the other's knee. After 30 minutes, Kania Ke said, "We need to go down the hill."

They got into the jeep and headed towards town. When they came to a crossroad, the Shaman said, "Stop". He then pointed towards the road on their left. " We go this way."

"Where are we going?" Shannon asked.

Kania Ke explained. "I see vision of quarry when in trance. It is a good place to search."

When they arrived in the Rana Roratka volcano area, they pulled off the road to the Rabu Raraku quarry.

The Mayan Shaman swept his arm toward the quarry. "This is place rock for statues on outer rim of island came. Here we find Stone."

"It is near another extinct volcano, so maybe our first insight about the volcano was right." Shannon glanced down at her hands as if contemplating what she was saying.

Isabel put her hands on her hips. "If this is so then we need to tune into where the Stone was hidden. May be a dubious task, eh?"

"We look for a spot where an adept might have gone to find the best hiding place for his Stone. What do you think, Kania Ke?"

The man swept his hand over the quarry area. "This is small. Not many places to hide such an object. Also, not much has happened here for many years." He pointed to a ledge that jutted out from the rest. "We try up there first."

When they got to the top of the ledge that was part of a huge quarry piece, Shannon stared down into a trough in the rock. "Wow. I would never have imagined this from down there."

"We should take a look." Isabel peeked first into the trough and then at the shaman. "What do you say Kania Ke?"

He nodded. "Of course, this is why we are here."

Isabel jumped into the shallow crevice, flipped on her light, and flashed it around the dark edges. She pointed towards the northern end. "This end continues that way. Let me try it." She crept along the trough on her hands and knees, shining her light ahead.

When she got to the end, a large opening appeared and seemed to drop off into a hole. Unable to crawl further, she turned back and reported what she had found.

"We wait." The man glanced around him. "If this one gives us something to explore, then more here. Let us explore." He turned and headed up the hill. The two women stared at each other and shrugged. When they reached the top the Shaman was climbing into a ravine. He disappeared for a few moments, and then popped back out of the ravine. "Dead end."

They explored three more similar areas with the same results. The man stared at the sky and said. "Sun low. We come back in the morning."

Shannon glanced at her watch. "We have only three more days. We must find the Stone soon."

He nodded. "Early morning, we return and find Stone. Promise." He smiled. Just as he stepped off of the mound he had been searching, the Shaman stopped. "Something here, I feel it. We must return to this place."

Shannon caught the man's gaze on their way to the jeep. "Why did you think the place we left was where we want to search?"

He smiled. "I feel a loving energy in one place on the ridge as it slopes. Also I get message. It said 'here'. Good sign."

They drove back to the hotel, and then discussed the Shaman's revelation over dinner.

The women smiled. "Sounds like we are close to our goal." Isabel said.

"May the morning sunlight shine upon our task." Shannon held up her cup. The other two touched their cups to hers.

The next morning, they hurried through breakfast, and then drove to the place they had left the previous day. It had rained and the spray from the tires reflected the sunlight, creating sparkling colors in their wake. When the explorers arrived, they grabbed some tools from the jeep, and climbed the hill to the intended spot.

In her hurry to get there, Isabel slipped on the wet slope and her heels dug into the earth displacing bits of soil and grass. When the other two got to the place that Kania Ke had mentioned the day before, he examined the smudge where Isabel had slipped just a few feet away.

"I sense something under this." The man pushed his small shovel into the loosened dirt from Isabel's boot. He dug deeper it, revealing a stone surface. They all used their shovels and uncovered a solid block of stone about a foot below the soil. They dug to the edges. "Someone put this here. It does not blend with the surrounding stone." He bent down and felt the edges. "We may need rope you brought to pull this away."

"Hold on." Shannon ran back to the jeep, and returned with a four foot shovel. "It was in the bottom of the jeep. We can use it to pry up the stone."

They dug out one end of the five foot long stone, put the shovel underneath, and pried it upward. They pushed rocks under the corner, and repeated the process for the next 30 minutes, until they were able to push the stone off of its base. Isabel shone her light into the rectangular opening.

The hole was just wide enough for Kania Ke to get into. He lowered himself beneath the surface until his shoes touched something hard about eight feet below. He used his light and scanned the area.

There seemed to be room for her, so Shannon climbed in too, and Isabel stayed on the surface to hand them things, and offer what help she could give from the top.

Inside the hole, Shannon flashed her light over the surfaces. In front of her there appeared to be a mixture of rock and dirt, but behind her sat a wall of stone. The Shaman was already examining the gray stone area with great care.

She turned and moved to where he was working. "We usually look for some inconsistency in the way the area is laid out. In caves, we look for pockets or niches. Have you noticed anything irregular in the wall?"

"Yes, here." He pointed to an area of a different color and texture than the surrounding stone. It felt smoother and was a lighter gray with a bit of white in it. "Does not match the rest of the surface. What do you think?"

Shannon examined it. "I think we need to dig into this with something." She pulled out a chisel and hammer from her daypack. Her first blow knocked a chip out from the surface, almost hitting the Shaman. After it landed a few feet away, Kania Ke said, "I feel energy." He came closer to the small indentation now exposed and peered into it. "Energy comes from here."

Shannon and the man worked on the area for another 20 minutes, chipping out small pieces of rock and what seemed like an aggregate of perhaps pumice and volcanic stone; definitely not natural. The chipping got easier the further they dug. Each time another large area of light gray rock was exposed, the energy increased.

Kani Ke put his ear to the exposed rock surface. "I hear someone." He pointed. "From in here."

"I think we have found your Wisdom Stone, Kania Ke." She kept chipping away until she broke through about a foot into the rock. The energy increased until Shannon could now feel it. "I feel an intense, but soft wave of energy pass through my hands."

Isabel yelled. "What is happening down there? I feel something."

"We are close to finding the Stone," said Shannon.

She changed the angle of her chisel, and then a large piece fell away. The Mayan reached inside the hole and pulled out a small, metal box. He unlatched the top, pulled it off and the area lit up. Shining from a leather pouch was a soft, violet light. The Shaman pulled the small bag from the container. "We are done. The Wisdom Stone is ours." He put the pouch back into the container without opening it, and put it in a pocket deep within his leather coat. The man put his hands up above the surface, and Isabel grabbed them pulling him up. She then helped Shannon.

"We must put this back the way we found it," said Shannon.

Kania Ke sat against the side of a mound for a few minutes, with the Stone close to his heart. They returned the slab across the hole and covered it with the dirt and grass. Satisfied that everything was returned to "normal", the three left the hill and returned to the jeep.

Shannon could tell that the Shaman and the Stone were conversing, so she had little to say to him about communication with the Wisdom Stone. They returned to the hotel, went to their rooms, and prepared for a late lunch. At 1:30 they met in the dining hall for their meal.

"Since we have plenty of light, we can begin our search for the Activation site." Shannon drank some tea.

Isabel gave her a puzzled look. "Is it not customary to give the Recipient plenty of time to communicate with the Stone?"

"Yes, that is how we have proceeded in the past, but tomorrow is the 11th. We must Activate the Wisdom Stone by sunset. So we have less time than usual, plus we have daylight for another five hours or so. I say we make good use of it."

The Shaman put his hand over his heart area. "I am told to seek many pools of water and go to the south. That would mean Rano Kau, the large extinct volcano at the south end of the island."

"Wow. Pretty precise info." Isabel sat back in the heavy chair sipping coffee.

Shannon smiled. "Yes, and we can pursue it now, not tomorrow."

"Greg found an underground waterway that led to a dry tunnel and cave at Chichen Itza. That is where we held the last Activation." Isabel said.

Shannon glanced at the Shaman. "We may need wet suits and tanks. That sound right to you?" He nodded.

They left the hotel, rented diving gear, and headed toward Rano Kau.

When they got into the jeep, Kania Ke said, "I am told we will need three more people here."

33

EASTER ISLAND

The three seekers donned their wetsuits and waded into the water
of Rano Kau. Pools of grass and willows greeted them. They had
to push past the plants to get to the clear water. After exploring
a 100 foot diameter circle, they came back together.

"The water only comes to my chest." Isabel said, being the tall-
est of the three. "I do not see a place to dive; but in Chichen Itza
Greg dug out a lot of debris collected over the years. Do you think
we need to do that here?"

The Mayan Shaman scrutinized the area. "I feel to go 'down'.
We search below and dig."

They spent an hour digging in different places, but found nothing. As they were making their way back to the shore to discuss the
situation, a young tourist called to them. "Why are you wearing
wetsuits in this warm, shallow water? The place to use them is
down there." He stood on a rim of the crater and pointed toward
the ocean below.

The three of them stared first at the man, and then at each
other. Shannon said, "Of course. What were we thinking? That is

what your 'go down' meant, Kania Ke." They slipped off their wet-suits and scuba gear, thanked the man, got into the jeep and drove around to where they had access to the ocean. They climbed down an embankment to within ten feet of the water.

Isabel jumped in first, and then the others followed. They searched around the volcano's wall that descended into the depths, trying to find an opening of some kind. They swam around the whole south end, and then almost 100 feet down, with no luck. They gathered at the jeep two hours later.

"After all it is a volcano. It rose out of the ocean and that is where its 'roots' go." Shannon shook her head. "It doesn't look promising."

Isabel stood. "Ha. I have seen less promising situations that turned out great. We just have to keep at it." She dove into the water and disappeared. *Maybe we have not gone down far enough. Or…wait, what is that?* As she swam downward and rounded a turn of the volcano's side, she spied a shadow-like vision. The closer she got the more it resembled a hole within a crevice. When she reached it, she shone her light into the hole. *This may be what we are looking for.*

She swam into the hole, and then upward for about 90 feet where it turned inward. Isabel followed the channel as it widened, and then turned upward again. Then, it split. *I need to go back and get the others.* She turned and made her way back to the opening that she marked by hammering a spike into the side of the hole, and then tying her tool belt from it. She raced to the top to tell Shannon and Kania Ke. When she got to the top, they had packed their suits into the jeep and sat waiting for her. The sun was low and it would be dark soon.

She strutted up the pathway to the jeep. "I have found an entrance."

Shannon gave her a startled look. "Oh? Where?" Isabel explained what she had found. "The sun is setting. It will be dark soon. We will look tomorrow."

"But I have only marked it with my tool belt." Isabel pleaded. "It will be gone by morning." She grabbed a rope from the vehicle, ran, to the water's edge, and jumped in. She swam down to where she had left her "marker", removed the belt, and tied one end of the rope to the spike. Isabel then swam back toward where Shannon and the Shaman awaited, but the rope ran out. She quickly tied the rope to one wrist, and then hammered another spike into the volcanic wall. She then tied the rope to it, and hoped it would hold until morning.

When she got back onto land, the sun had set and it was almost dark. She hopped into the vehicle, and off they rode toward the hotel. When they arrived, they made their way to their rooms, and met for their evening meal an hour later.

The group discussed their possible moves in the morning over a sumptuous local meal. Where they were led in the morning would make the difference of finding the Activation site before sunset, or missing the required "drop dead" timeslot and fail.

"I have a reply from Emily," Shannon said. "They will be here not later than tomorrow afternoon. Hopefully, in plenty of time to join us for the Activation."

Isabel smiled. "What a wonderful message you got from Spirit Kania Ke; bring all of us together for the finale Activation."

"I am always led to the best outcome for all concerned." The Mayan Shaman smiled. "Great Mystery shines its Light on me."

34

MUNICH, GERMANY

A drab, gray sky hung over Munich, Germany and Fitzburg's headquarters. The long mahogany table looked bare to Halmar Fitzburg, while he drank his beer. "Where are all my comrades? What is happening here?" The three men he brought back from Russia shared his discomfort.

"We must regroup, General." Gavin leaned forward. "Your other men will be released soon. The authorities cannot hold them long without a trial."

Halmar leaned back into the heavy maple chair. "Yes, you are right. But it is so disturbing." He paused and drank some amber colored ale. "I have good news though. I got a notice from the guy Karl in Sedona. He said they are closing the classroom in Madrid. It will be their first closing. Notice the word 'first'. It appears we have convinced them that they can not win; all they can do is fight us off when we attack. But still…"

One of the other men got up, and then paced the room. "I sense uneasiness, but am wondering why we are not celebrating. First, we destroy one of those powerful stones, ending their ability to continue with their project. Then, we finally convince them to stop teaching and shut down their classrooms. Am I missing something?"

Fitzburg and the other two men stared at Franko; each one seemingly in deep thought. After a minute of silence Halmar responded. "Yes, Franko, I agree. It is just that the work of getting to this point has been longer and more intense than I had projected. It seemed we could easily stop three people untrained in military combat. Instead, we ran up against Martial Artists who kicked our asses. Even when you three threatened them with weapons, they did the same. I was not expecting that. By God we are military veterans, we should rule." He banged his fist on the table so hard that his personalized stein of beer bounced and almost fell over.

The other three men flinched and raised their eyebrows, startled at the outburst. The room fell silent for a few minutes. Fitzburg arose, picked up his stein and saw it was empty. "Yes, we need to celebrate; but I have this gut feeling that more is going on than we are aware of. Have you ever felt like things were going the way you wanted them to, but deep down had this foreboding feeling?" He glanced at the three men, who first stared at their mugs, and then looked at each other.

Franko gripped his mug tightly and said, "Well, yes General I guess we all have at one time or another. I cannot at this time, however share that feeling with you. I understand what you are saying, and suggest we not necessarily conclude that we have absolutely won. We will continue to watch them and listen to their communications for any sign of trickery."

"That we can do for sure," said Fitzburg, "and when the rest of my men return, we will all take some time off. I will advise my comrades to continue their surveillance and send me the data. Right now, let us adjourn to the pub downtown."

35

EASTER ISLAND

On the morning of 11-11-2011, the sun cast a shimmering rainbow over Rano Kau. The night before had been colder than normal, and when the heat of the sun hit the pools of water in the volcano's crater, a mist rose above it. But Shannon preferred her perspective. "Look – a rainbow; right above Rano Kau. Is that not a sign for our success?"

The group viewed the rainbow with reverence, and discarded any scientific explanation. The magnificent rainbow at this moment of their search for an Activation site could not be a coincidence. The three adventurers hugged, and loaded their gear into the jeep. Their last day to find the site and Activate the Wisdom Stone had come; it was now or never.

When they arrived at the place they had left the night before, something seemed different. The tide was higher and covered much of the area where they had parked the jeep, but also the place from which Isabel surfaced had disappeared. That is, when she surfaced at dusk, a rounded corner helped her find the way to the jeep. But the wall now looked almost straight.

Isabel put her foot into the water. "Did the tide rise that much? The curved wall and pebbly ground I used to get back here are covered." She ran her hand over the wall.

"Twenty to thirty feet of road is under water compared to last night." The Shaman pointed to the area behind the jeep.

Shannon said, "Yes, the tide has risen a lot. Remember the full moon last night."

As Isabel waded into the water her foot caught something. She jumped back in case it was a snake of some kind. When it did not move she bent down and grabbed it. "Oh my god, it is my rope." She pulled the limp rope from the water and held it up. "The whole thing came undone. Now we have no marker as to where the hole I found might be. Ahg!" She rolled it up and tied it to her pack. "So much for your 'good luck' rainbow."

Shannon finished donning her wetsuit and came to the water's edge. "I see your point. Still, everything happens for a reason. Maybe something is telling us to look in another direction."

"Yeah, maybe something is just making it harder to complete our mission." Isabel frowned.

Kania Ke came to where the two women stood. "Water rise maybe 10 feet. Not that much, but enough to make a difference of where we search. We look first at what was <u>not</u> under water when we first explored."

"Good point." Shannon turned to Isabel. "What do you think?"

Isabel turned toward the wall. "Yeah, sure. I guess we check out what was above water last night." She put on her mask and dove into the water.

The other two followed her. The three then split up, each taking a section of the previously above-the-water wall area. After about 90 minutes of searching for an entrance of some kind, they surfaced at about the distance from the shore that they had explored the previous evening. They hung on to a large root. "I find nothing." Isabel shouted.

"No, me either," said Shannon.

The Shaman lifted his mask. He pointed toward the west and the northern curve of the volcano; beyond where they had previously looked. "We need to go that way." They all dove back into the water and repeated the procedure in the new areas.

Thirty minutes later Shannon, who was at the top of the receding water line, waved for Isabel and Kania Ke to come to where she hung in the water against the wall. When they got there she pointed to the outline of crack circling a notch halfway above the water. "This crack encircles the notch and there is a knobby protrusion on one side. I think with some persuasion this could come loose."

Treading water and hanging onto the protrusion, Isabel began chipping away with hammer and chisel. The others joined her. The notch moved somewhat the deeper they dug into the crack. Then all three grabbed what they could of the knob and pulled it toward the opposite side, their feet against the wall. Each tug on the knob caused the notch to loosen until it left the wall. Water rushed into the now opened crevice and almost pulled them with it. Then it stopped.

The opened crevice was now just a few inches above the water, and almost three feet in diameter. Since Shannon was the smallest of the three, she moved into the hole first. After swimming in a downward direction for 100 feet, the cavity turned upward about 20 degrees and widened. Above the turn, the water leveled and a cavern appeared. Shannon turned around in the wider air space and swam back out.

She lifted her mask and took a deep breath. "We have found a way into the volcano. It appears similar to what you described last night Isabel. Maybe the entrances are connected."

One at a time, the three swam into the crevice and proceeded into the wider section. They removed their breathing gear and began their passage into a tunnel. It continued to widen and get higher as they crawled on the cold lava floor. "This is beginning to look like a lava tube that Greg described when he searched for his Wisdom Stone on the Big Island in Hawaii two years ago." Shannon said.

"Yes, it looks similar to what I saw below us yesterday." Isabel touched the walls.

Kania Ke shone his light ahead of them. "We are in the right place. The one below is a similar creation by the lava's movement. They may somehow be connected, but it is of no concern to us now. We must move forward."

As they moved through the tube, it got tall enough for them to stand upright, but with Isabel's head brushing the ceiling. The cave, or lava tube, leveled out and remained that way the rest of their trek. Even though the tube turned several times, they had no way of telling which direction they faced when they arrived at the end, opening into a larger cavity.

"Oh my god, it looks surreal and beautiful," said Shannon.

Stalactites hung from the ceiling, some containing what looked like crystals as the light from their lanterns struck them. Each of the three lit a different part of the cave, revealing more of the sparkling crystals. Then, they all focused on one spot in the center, due to its unique and unbelievable structure. A rounded stalagmite looked like a small table and was surrounded by twelve similar structures.

"It looks likes a table and twelve chairs." Isabel touched each one. "How is this possible?"

The Mayan Shaman touched them also. "We are led. There is no other explanation. This is the Activation site. These unique and mysterious formations will serve in their own special way during the Activation ceremony. Each one has taken its own form to serve this final ceremony's legacy." He turned toward the others. "You must go meet and bring your friends. They are here. I will stay and prepare the site. I need fire; bring me a lighter."

"I will stay with Kania Ke as a guard." Isabel turned to Shannon. "I will follow you to the entrance with a rope. The tide is dropping, and the four of you will need to climb up to the hole. When you arrive I will lower it. You can use you're your phone, but doubt it will work in this cavern. Bring some snacks. I'm hungry." She smiled.

It was now 4:00 p.m. The sun would set at about 7:00. Shannon had to meet Emily, Greg, and Karl, and get them wet suits. She had already rented diving gear, lights, air tanks, and more lights for themselves the night before. Once finished getting the added equipment, lighter, and snacks, they would have to get back to the Activation site before 7:00.

When Isabel and Shannon reached the small tunnel or what they called the "turn around place", they noticed the water had receded. Shannon crawled to the entrance and observed that the water level had fallen three feet or so, since they left it two hours before. She crawled back to the "turn around place" grabbed one end of the rope, and then crawled out of the entrance. When she reached the water, she put on her mask and headed to shore. Isabel pulled up the rope, glanced at her watch, and headed back to the Activation chamber.

Shannon swam close to the volcano's wall to make sure she would get back on the road close to the jeep. When she got there, Shannon took off her wet suit, jumped in the jeep, and took off toward the airport. When she arrived, she found Emily sitting on her suitcase and leaning against a pole.

"Hi Emily, it is so great to see you again." They hugged. "Where are Greg and Karl?"

Emily laughed. "I think they needed food."

As Shannon and Emily began loading the luggage in the jeep, the men arrived and helped. "Hello, my dear Shannon." Karl gave her a long hug.

Greg said "hi" and jumped in the back of the vehicle with Emily. "We have some shopping to do, but let's first get you checked in at the hotel so we can unload these suitcases." Shannon said.

After leaving the hotel, they drove to the dive shops to rent suits. They then picked up a few snacks and threw them in a water-proof sack. Shannon bought the fire-starter lighter asked for by the Shaman.

"What is that for?" Asked Greg.

Shannon shrugged. "I don't know. Kania Ke requested it."

"Must have something to do with the Activation," said Emily.

On the way to water's edge, Shannon filled them in on what had taken place since the discovery of the Wisdom Stone. "Wow, lava tubes. Takes me back a couple of years." Greg smiled.

"The calling for all of us to be present for the Activation reminds me of the similar gathering when we activated the seventh Stone." Emily spread out her arms. "I remember all of us gathered in a circle, when the last two came in and sat with us. It seemed like Spirit thanking all of the participants for a job well done."

Shannon smiled. "Yes, it was so exciting. Thank you for allowing me to be part of this last Stone search and Activation. I feel honored."

"We were honored to have you and Isabel fill in when we had other things going on." Emily touched Shannon's shoulder. Karl smiled.

When they arrived at the end of the road, Shannon called Isabel's satellite phone, but got no response. They all donned their wetsuits, gathered their gear, and followed Shannon into the water. They kept close to Shannon so as not to lose sight of her. When she got to the rendezvous point with Isabel, Shannon swam to the top and clung on to the side of the wall, while the others treaded water. She shouted for Isabel, but got no answer.

Where is she? It's been over two hours since I left. The sun is setting. Where is she? Shannon swam out from the wall to assure herself that the hole was above her. She saw the hole but no Isabel. She returned to the wall, turned toward the others, shook her head, and put up her arms. The rest of them found places on the volcano's wall to hang from.

They all hung around, literally, for another ten minutes when the end of a rope hit Shannon on the head. She glanced up and smiled. *At last.* She grabbed the end, wrapped it around her waist, and then with Isabel's help, pulled herself up the side of the volcano's wall. When she got to the hole, Shannon crawled into the almost dry tunnel to where Isabel awaited her.

"Where have you been?" Shannon wrinkled her brow.

Isabel shrugged. "It's complicated, I'll explain later. Let's get the others up. Here is how it will work. I will stay here and help with the next person, but then I will go on up to the next level, as two people cannot fit in the tunnel nor where we stand. Pass this on to the next person. I suggest it be Karl, since there are two of us here to help pull him up."

"Got it." Shannon then crawled out and yelled to the others that Karl would go next and threw down the rope. Once he got it tied around his waist, she signaled to Isabel and the two of them pulled, while Karl did his best to get himself up. When he got to the hole, he crawled in to where Shannon now stood in the alcove. She explained how to do the turn around. He did so and then crawled back out to the entrance.

Isabel and Shannon left and waited at the top, where they had more room. After another 30 minutes, they all gathered in the larger part of the lava tube in single file, but standing. "We have a ways to go like this, but it gets wider." Isabel said, and led the way with a steady fast pace. "We really need to push it. It is already close to Activation time and the Shaman needs that lighter."

36

ACTIVATION

Twenty minutes after Shannon and the others had gathered in the lava tube, they arrived in the large chamber, now the Activation site. Kania Ke was busy attending to twelve candles, one on each "stool" around the 'table'. A violet light lit the altar that now held the Pale Violet Stone resting upon a piece of rough wood, and surrounded by what looked like seaweed. The light spread throughout the room and continued to get brighter. Shannon gave him the lighter and he bowed to her. Everyone removed their wetsuits and stowed them and their gear along the wall, out of the way.

The Mayan raised his arms and then lowered them pointing to the floor. Everyone sat around the altar area and waited quietly. The violet light increased its brightness, and then was joined by a bright White Light that spread energy throughout the room. Above the Violet Stone hung a being of Light.

"Greetings from the realm of the Mayan Ancestors. My name is Archivale. It is my esteemed pleasure to serve you. Tonight we close the gate to the unification of powerful and sacred Stones of Wisdom. It is their time to radiate spiritual energy throughout your world. While many of the Ancients, Ascended Masters, Angels, and Archangels have already begun lifting the veils that have kept us separated, these Stones will finish this undertaking. Long have we awaited this day.

I welcome all of you, who one might call saviors; for you have risked much to bring this time to your world. But you have persevered, even fought bravely to continue your task, when those who do not have as clear a vision as you tried to stop your Missions. Tonight we honor you as you bear witness to this final Activation. Let us begin."

"Kania Ke has already prepared the room for our event. The Pale Violet Stone rests upon an ancient piece of driftwood he collected from the volcanic pools below us, and ocean grass surrounds it. He has washed them with water both from the pools and the ocean that I purified when we readied them for this ceremony. Around them all are twelve candles made from the wax of bees, supported by sand from the ocean's floor and the volcanic lava below the pools. These articles represent Earth, Water, Vegetation, and Wood, all natural elements of your planet. We will add Fire to this mix in a moment. But now, I add Air."

Archivale blew upon the unlit candles and then around the room, filling it with loving energy. "Before Kania Ke lights each candle, we sing, for sound is but another sacred element we enjoy. We are joined by Angels who will fill our hearts to overflowing with love." The room burst into angelic voices coming from every direction. Everyone joined the singing by dancing around the room adding their voices to the jubilation. The singing lasted about 20 minutes, and then slowly and quietly subsided. They sat again and the room fell silent.

After a short time, Archivale spoke again. "We are now ready to begin the ceremony of acknowledging our blessed Wisdom Stones. The first seven candles will represent the seven sacred Wisdom Stones Activated two years ago." He turned towards Kania Ke, who stood in front of the first candle. While the candle seemed white, it had a violet glow about it.

"Light this first candle, honoring the Violet Stone that Greg Activated so reverently. It called forth the Violet Ray and Faith." Emily turned toward Greg and smiled. He just nodded. *"We know that Faith is the foundation of the unexplained in your world, for without it, your view of the world is one of little substance much like the sea where you can find no foothold and so sink into the void. The Violet Ray brings forth purity and Divinity. Its Divine Substance purifies whatever it strikes, cleansing your lives when used."*

"Light the second candle." Kania Ke bowed and lit the candle. He then backed away. It gave off a blue aura to the room. *"This candle honors the Blue Wisdom Stone Activated by Terra, a wise Shaman indeed. This Stone brings forth Spiritual Understanding and the Blue Ray of inspiration and creativity. Spiritual Understanding opens the human mind and connects it to all minds, which are in Oneness with Great Spirit. The Blue Ray inspires your creativity so you can communicate on a higher level, and sets the space for you to speak your truth."*

"Light the third candle." The Mayan lit the third candle that seemed to glow a light green color. *"This candle honors the Green Stone Activated by Gorges. It called forth the Green Ray and Divine Love. The Green Ray activates one's heart center; the most powerful area of the human body. The Green Ray's energy permeates all that it touches with peace, love, and healing. The Stone's energy of Divine Love falls upon humanity who knows little of its power. But when this sacred Force caresses the human heart and it is felt by this world, Divine Love will be known."*

"Light the fourth candle." The Shaman stepped forward and lit the candle that emanated a bright white glow. *"This candle honors the White Stone Activated by Shannon, and calls the Bright White Ray and Acceptance."* Shannon's and Karl's eyes met, and they smiled. *"It opens the human mind to see beyond what appears to be, to what really is. With this revealing information you can now accept the situation or person for what or who they really are. The Bright White Ray is the light of God that shines upon each one of you even if you do not know it."*

The cavern seemed brighter and more open when the voice grew quiet. After a few minutes of silence, he spoke again.

"Light the fifth candle." Again, the Mayan touched the wick of the candle, which now gave off a pink glow. *"This candle honors the pale pink Stone and the Pale-Pink Ray of Forgiveness Activated by Jasmine. This is a most needed energy for your planet. When you live in Fear, the only way to begin healing what Fear brings is through Forgiveness. Here, forgiveness is about seeing beyond appearances to what is Real, and then embracing this vision for the condition you are experiencing, letting go of false beliefs."*

"Light the sixth candle." Kania Ke stepped forth and lit the sixth candle. Immediately, the candle was surrounded by a glowing turquoise mist. *"This candle honors the Turquoise Stone and the Pale-Turquoise Ray of Harmony Activated by Chris. This Ray helps restore balance to the imbalanced condition by restoring harmony where disharmony exists. It also establishes vibrations within the body that begins the process of re-balancing and harmony."*

Music and vibrations moved through the room evoking a harmonious feeling in the group. Karl squeezed Shannon's hand. When the room grew quiet again, Archivale spoke.

"Light the seventh candle." The Shaman moved gently to the circle and lit the candle. It immediately took on a bright orange light radiating from it. *"This candle honors the final Stone of the seven, Activated two years ago by Rampur. This orange colored Stone brings forth Wisdom and the Orange Ray. The ancients, and even present day awakened beings have given you wisdom to live by, but sadly it is missed by most of your world. Most humans depend solely on the intellect, and it has its place, but unless it is tempered by wisdom, you are lost. Call upon this Ray when wisdom is needed."*

Archivale addressed everyone in the circle. "You wise beings of love thought it finished when you left Lhasa, but recently discovered five more blessed Wisdom Stones were meant to join the others. And so here we are at the real completion of this journey."

"Please light the eighth candle." Kanni Ke reached over and lit the candle, which shone a soft red light all around it.

"This candle honors the red Stone and the Red Ray of Life that Master Wu Activated. The Life-force moves through your bodies, it allows you to identify with your spiritual nature, rather than having the energy flow outwards toward the sensory world. Even though the director of the Life-force is the ego, which governs the body's life and generative functions, the body still maintains its spiritual presence. It is this function that really runs your life." The red glowing light moved through the room and awakened the Life-force in each person. Greg felt a loving sensation in his root chakra and knew it was this energy.

"We move on now to the ninth Stone. Light this candle please." The Shaman gently lit the wick and a golden glow mixed with silver surrounded the candle and the flame. *"This candle honors the Golden-Silver Stone of Honor, Activated by Niki. Honor lifts you high in wholeness. It melds integrity and respect. Honor touches the depth of your Being, releasing this union. You reach out, and as you honor others, you honor yourself. Honoring all of Life and treating it with respect, brings it to you and becomes a part of you. You will then move about the Earth with Honor, in Honor."*

"This is a most gracious Stone, because it allows each of us to honor the other. And so I honor each of you sitting here tonight, for you have taken on a great challenge, fought off your adversaries with great respect, and completed your Missions in grace."

Greg thought about his experience with The Cause and his ability to honor them. He searched deep within himself. A spark of respect and honor came forth, because even though they seemed cruel he knew they only acted out of fear. They did what they believed to be right based on their beliefs and knowledge.

"Let us now move on to the tenth candle." Kania Ke got up, smiling, for he had been honored many times, but never with others that accompanied him, as those with him now. He lit the tenth candle that began to glow with a pale yellow light.

"This candle honors the Stone of Vision and the Yellow Ray Activated by Shali. The visionary looks not backward at what might have been, but eternally forward at what can be. It is with great Vision that ancient Prophets and Masters have foretold what was to come.

The Master Jesus said: 'These things that I do, you also can do . . . and even more.' Did he not give you the Secret, in just that one sentence? Your Vision is your life. Without it you crumble as clay when it dries."

"Your vision of a kinder, gentler world will come, dear ones. After tonight, all of the Stones will begin merging, and complete that action on 12-21-2012. Stay with it. You will see. Let us now light the eleventh candle."

The Mayan arose, bent over and lit the candle. It then emitted a pink glow surrounded by a golden ring of light. *"This candle honors the Stone of Compassion, and the Golden-Pink Ray, activated by Carlos. Compassion is Unconditional Love in action. All the Great Masters taught us to reach for Love and that embracing Love was the root of human existence. You are all one human family living together upon a planet that supports your Oneness. Surely Compassion lifts both the giver and receiver to a new level of understanding. The Golden-Pink Ray will maintain your level of Compassion and bring Oneness closer."*

"Now, my friends, we come to the final Activation. The one that will set in motion all that I have described tonight. Kania Ke, please prepare your Pale-Violet Stone for its Activation."

"Take some water now and drop it on the sea grass."

Kania Ke did so and the grass grew around the Pale-Violet Stone, like a crown.

"Now some water on the ancient wood." He let more water drop upon the driftwood on which the Stone sat. It expanded and raised the Stone above the grass "crown", until it now looked like a ribbon around the "pedestal", which held the Stone.

"And finally, let some water drop upon the Pale-Violet Stone."

When Kania Ke droped the water onto the Stone, Pale-Violet light blazed from it and spread out into the room. It touched the ceiling and the walls. Each person felt its energy and settled into a feeling of peace and love.

Music once again sounded throughout the room and Angelic voices sang of Love. While it lasted everyone danced and sang with it. When it stopped, they all sat once again.

"Please light the twelfth candle."

The man quietly and gently touched the flame to the wick. When lit, the Stone sent forth another wave of Pale-Violet energy throughout the room, touching everyone.

"This beautiful violet Stone calls the Pale-Violet Ray of Transcendence into our midst and into your world. It marks the pinnacle of spiritual achievement for the human race. When one transcends that which no longer serves, he or she moves beyond what you call the ego and seems to fly. The freedom that follows transcendence cannot be described, but only felt.

Each of the earlier Activations put forth a challenge to all Earthly inhabitants. And each must be Transcended, before Spiritual Mastery is achieved. But what does that mean? To Transcend something is to move beyond its bounds, and then look back to know it is finished. And so when Love is transcended it does not mean that one moves beyond Love, for Love is all there is, but to move beyond what keeps a being from experiencing this energy of Love. Transcendence allows the being to no longer find his or her world unacceptable, or think themselves above, or below, another, but to move beyond and humbly live with All of Life.

Transcendence is the final mark of achievement in human endeavor. It moves the achiever to Mastery. Great Masters like Buddha and Jesus transcended their world and saw a greater one beyond. They knew that they were not of their world but only in it. Yes, in it for a short while to serve, as are you, my friends. Service to The One Source of All, service to the Earth, service to each other and to all of life is surely your destinies. Sharing this world with all those upon it in a loving, compassionate, and peaceful way points to your service."

"Those that would 'see the Light' are in need of your service, for they would leave the darkness if they only they knew how. This final Activation binds the other eleven in a Ring of Love around the Earth. All twelve Stones bring Transcendence to the fore and are illuminated by it."

The room grew silent. A wave of violet light energy spread throughout the cavern and touched each person. The colored lights from all twelve candles first spread throughout the room, and then came together with a rainbow effect. Kania Ke spread his arms out feeling the transcendent energy move through him. He felt his Shamanic powers expand beyond what he had ever known; it was if he had been lifted to a new level. He felt Oneness with all of life.

Then Archivale spoke for the last time. "It is finished. All twelve Wisdom Stones are connected. It will take 13 months for their combined energy to reach its pinnacle, but the energy will continue to grow from this moment onward. When 12-12-2012 happens, great amounts of spiritual energy will have built within the twelve Wisdom Stone vortex. From that point on all the peoples of the earth will become a part of it. This energy opens a door for the transition to a new Age on 12-21-2012; the end of the Mayan calendar as you know it, and the beginning of the Golden Age of Humanity. The Illumination of the twelve Wisdom Stones will light up your world like it has never before seen."

"Humans on this planet will begin to see each other for who they are. They will begin to live in Oneness with all of life. You have given much to the world and it will give the same and much more, back to you. I bid each of you Love, Peace, and Divine Power. You have served well. Continue your Sacred Work." With that, Archivale disappeared and the room grew quiet in the glow of the burning candles.

Everyone in the room stood and hugged each other. Then one by one, shook the others' hand, congratulating them for adding to this completion of almost two years of work. They left the same way they arrived at the cavern. When the last person left the room, and that was Greg, a rumble sounded behind him and the opening closed with rock and lava particles sealing it. The Activation was indeed finished.

EPILOGUE

Later at the hotel restaurant on Easter Island, Greg stood, picked up the bottle of champagne he had ordered, and filled each glass around the table. He then held his glass high. "Tonight we celebrate, as Archivale said earlier, two years of elation, struggle, challenges, and successes; but most of all, two years of companionship, love, and camaraderie to finish a mission of worldwide importance." They all stood, clicked their glasses together, smiled, and then cheered.

"I want to honor our final Recipient and powerful Shaman, Kania Ke for such a great job and excellent choices the past few days." Shannon said, holding up her glass. They all cheered and thanked him for his work.

The Mayan Shaman stood. "You and Isabel have honored me in many ways during our venture together, but tonight, as I felt my Shamanic powers grow to that of Mastery, I was humbled. Thank you."

"Greg, Karl, and I thank you for inviting us to experience this final Activation." Emily said with tears running down her cheeks.

"When Greg got the idea to have Isabel and Shannon finish the Mission, we never though we would physically see the end. We are most grateful."

They spent the evening basking in the wonderment of fulfilling their Mission, and knew they had finally completed the task they thought they had finished two years before with great joy.

In the year following the twelfth Activation, many changes took place amongst our heroes and villains. After closing their classrooms in Sedona, Madrid, and Mt. Shasta the group of Wisdom Stone seekers disbanded.

Shannon and Karl moved to Magdalena, Mexico, a small town of 18,000, where they opened a new teaching center. They so enjoyed teaching classes together, and the wonderful people all around them.

Emily and Greg moved near Seattle, Washington, where Greg had previously worked and lived. They opened two teaching centers - one in Yakima, and the other near their home. Greg got back to writing, in between his teaching sessions.

Isabel moved back to Rome, but then decided to join Shannon in Mexico as the promised 2012 Wisdom Stone activity neared. She would help Karl open a second center, help with translations, and being a Spanish interpreter.

The group directed by Halmar Fitzburg disbanded, satisfied they had stopped the "satanic" teachings, after confirming the closings of the centers (classrooms), and the disappearances of Emily, Greg, and the rest. Fitzburg retired from his military position and rejoined his family in Munich, Germany.

Kent moved back to the United States and got a job driving a truck.

Friedrick moved back to Rome, Italy and found employment in a bar.

The rest of Fitzburg's men stayed in or near Munich and got odd jobs to keep them out of trouble.

Monsignor Terkenni served another year in prison and then was released on probation. Defrocked of this ministerial role in the Catholic Church, <u>Mr</u>. Terkenni attended regularly seeking forgiveness and healing.

The rest of the world began to 'wake up' again as the first seven Wisdom Stones increased their energies once more, and the second five Stones began to send out their energies. People became more connected, happier, and interested in spiritual principles.

Emily, Greg, Shannon, Karl, and Isabel had decided to gather in Sedona, Arizona for the 12-21-2012 final merging of all twelve Stones' energy. We join them now while they await this event.

The group enjoyed their evening meal in the resort's dining room knowing it was merely a precursor to the exciting event planned for the next day. Tonight they celebrated their reunion after almost a year apart, and catching up on what had transpired the past ten months.

"How are you enjoying Magdalena?" Emily asked.

Shannon smiled. "Oh, it is wonderful. It is small, although bigger than Sedona, only two hours away from the border, and about 160 klicks to the Gulf of California. The teaching center there is doing well, and we are opening one in Santa Ana, just down the road a bit. What about your place in Washington?"

"Well, it surely isn't Sedona; wet, and cold much of the time." Greg wrinkled his brow. "I remember many reasons why I had left the place five years ago. But we are up in the hills, away from the big cities and fairly dry, at least more so than near the water. We moved there just to get away from Sedona's environment for awhile. The two teaching centers that we setup are growing, especially the one in Yakima."

Karl laughed. "Yeah, I remember all the complaints when we were looking for Stones. 'I don't like the cold, give me a warm, dry place to search'. And here you are again."

"Yeah, but not for rest of my life." Greg smiled. "We will move down south in a year or two, when things get going well in the two centers." He turned to Isabel. "What made you move from your flat in Rome?"

Isabel took a sip of espresso. "I just grew tired of the place, been there most of my life. I thought a stint in Mexico would give me new perspectives. So far, I enjoy it. It may change. We will see."

Emily noted that they would meet at 8:00 a.m. for their celebration of the twelve Stones' Illumination. Even though the Solstice would occur at 4:11 a.m. Arizona time, they had selected 8:00 a.m. to hold the celebration, since the dining hall would not open until then. They would meet in a private room of the dining hall.

Shannon and Emily had gathered some candles, crystals, decorative ribbons and crape flourishes. The five of them then embellished the meeting room they had rented. After the decorations were complete, they alerted a few people they had met at the resort, and some friends from Sedona, about the celebration in the morning. They finished their evening with more chatter and toasts, and then retired for the night.

The next morning at 4:00 a.m. the five of them gathered in Emily and Greg's room and seated themselves in a circle holding hands. They closed their eyes and awaited the energy. Soon, each felt warmth, peace, and love within their hearts. It went far beyond what they had ever felt before. It was as if moonlight, sunlight, and the wind all swept across their bodies at once.

They stayed in the circle for about 20 minutes, feeling as though their bodies had lifted from the soft carpet and hung in the air. Then, they got up hugged each other and quietly returned to their rooms.

The five friends assembled in the meeting room at 8:00 a.m. with their guests. They sat around a large, round table and grew quiet. They all held hands, closed their eyes, breathed into their hearts, and waited.

Within ten minutes of the group's gathering around the table, Emily and Shannon began to feel strong, loving energy move through their bodies again, like a summer breeze. Soon, Greg, Karl, and Isabel felt it as well. Greg could tell when the person's hand on either side of him grew warm and energy from them moved through his as well.

Those gathered remained in their positions for another 30 minutes, and then Emily said, "It is finished," feeling that the energy they felt earlier had completed its integration. They all opened their eyes, got up, smiled, laughed, and hugged one another. From then on, the room took on a cheery mood like a family celebration as breakfast was served. The rest of the day was spent in merriment, much like a day at a festival.

The energies shared by this group were also felt by people around the world in many different ways. A couple in Paris, France were arguing when suddenly they stopped, peered deeply into each other's eyes, and then hugged.

A woman in the middle of delivering twins was having a difficult time birthing her first baby. Then in a matter of seconds he came out easily. The next baby followed her brother effortlessly.

In four different places around the world, raging wars suddenly stopped. Soldiers turned to each other, and in tears embraced one another.

These kinds of events happened within minutes of the Solstice, for that is when the twelve Stones' energy merged completely. People everywhere called them miracles.

While a new cycle of time was also being born, the Stones' energy increased their presence to everyone. What great foresight those wise beings had four hundred years ago, planning to have the twelve Stones merge at this historic time in human history.

How blessed was the world for peace was at last in sight. Oneness would grow and separateness would end; it might take years, but the process had started and could not be stopped.

ABOUT THE AUTHOR

In addition to writing, Art Ramsay's current practice involves working as a Minister of Peace, a Spiritual (Peace) Coach, and seminar facilitator. He has studied and practiced Spiritual Principles for twenty-five years and brings those experiences to his writing. Through Art's work with people over the years through seminars and classes, he found that there are certain aspects of the human psyche that brings stress and a great deal of despair to our daily lives. His writing reflects bringing the awareness of those aspects to his readers in a way that promotes transformation, and incorporating what works in their lives. If, through  reading his books, a person's life is touched in a way that allows inner reflection, then he feels he has fulfilled his purpose.

In his first book of fiction, Seven Stones of Wisdom, Art brings forth seven spiritual principles that if applied to our everyday experience, would change us forever. By creating a book of fiction, he believes that people can be made aware of spiritual principles in a fun and interesting way. Following characters in a book is a way to see how those characters' lives change through applying what they learn in the story.

His second book, The Tibetan Wisdom Code, continues the story with a twist. The discovery of a mysterious coded document must be found to bring the dying Stones back to life. Again, lessons in spiritual practice are laced throughout the book, more in the form of classroom sessions than through the Wisdom Stones.

This third book of the trilogy, Illumination Of The Stones, will finish The Mission begun in Seven Stones of Wisdom. We hear from the Wisdom Stones again passing on to us more understanding from which to live our lives. We also gain knowledge through the seminars featured in the story, and wise beings met along the way.

Mr. Ramsay has also written a non-fiction eBook on Inner Peace that takes a no-nonsense look at what we must do to find and live a peaceful and harmonious life. You can find more out at:

http://www.innerpeacerevealed.com

Art lives in Asheville, North Carolina amongst the beautiful Smoky and Appalachian mountains with his wife, Dee, their dog, Shelby and cat, Hopi. He loves hiking in the beautiful mountains, kayaking in lakes nearby, and enjoys a close connection to nature and Mother Earth.

Art can be reached at
828-683-8661 or by e-mail at: art@innerpeaceandwisdom.com

More About the Wisdom Stones Trilogy

Seven Stones Of Wisdom
ISBN#978-0-9742776-7-7
© 2007, Rampart Press

Seven Stones Of Wisdom

An adventure into the human spirit racing a ticking clock and determined adversaries. Hidden at Sacred Sites centuries ago, powerful Wisdom Stones are awaiting discovery. Each Stone has a message of planetary significance to reveal and to set in motion spiritual transformation; seven sacred sited to explore, seven messages to transform humankind.

Can all seven stones be found and activated?

The World awaits its own transformation.

The Tibetan Wisdom Code
ISBN#978-0-9715946-7-8
© October 2011,
Magic Mountain Press

The Tibetan Wisdom Code

Two years have passed since the thrilling conclusion of the first book. This volume picks up the story and never slows its pace.

From monasteries in Tibet to the vortices in Sedona and ancient streets of Rome, an exciting spiritual adventure awaits!

The Stones are losing their power.

An ancient coded document in Tibet holds the key, as the lines between fact and fiction blur and our team of adventurers must unravel the clues.

All three books of the Wisdom Stones Trilogy can be purchased at:
Art's Inner Peace Site: *www.innerpeaceandwisdom.com/products.htm*

The first two books can also be found at:
Bookstores in Asheville, Waynesville, & Sylva, North Carolina, or

order a copy from your favorite bookstore!

Check online retailers.

www.ingramcontent.com/pod-product-compliance
Lightning Source LLC
Chambersburg PA
CBHW060315260626
47160CB00007B/2622